THE REFLECTION

ALSO BY HUGO WILCKEN

The Execution

David Bowie's Low (33 1/3)

Colony

THE REFLECTION

HUGO WILCKEN

A NOVEL

MELVILLE HOUSE
BROOKLYN • LONDON

THE REFLECTION

Copyright © 2015 by Hugo Wilcken

First Melville House printing: September 2015

Melville House Publishing   Melville House UK
            46 John Street   and   8 Blackstock Mews
        Brooklyn, NY 11201   Islington, London N4 2BT
mhpbooks.com   facebook.com/mhpbooks   @melvillehouse

Library of Congress Cataloging-in-Publication Data

Wilcken, Hugo, 1964–

The reflection : a novel / Hugo Wilcken.

pages ; cm

ISBN 978-1-61219-449-3 (hardcover)

ISBN 978-1-61219-450-9 (ebook)

I. Title.

PR9619.4.W55R44 2017

823'.92—dc23

2015010444

Design by Adly Elewa

Printed in the United States of America

10 9 8 7 6 5 4 3 2 1

PART ONE

I

"David Manne?"

"Speaking."

"Jeff Speelman here. I guess you may not remember me . . ."

"Why wouldn't I? How'd you get my number?"

"Looked it up in the phone book."

"What do you want?"

"It's about Abby."

"Jeff, I don't know what you could possibly say that would interest me. I haven't seen or spoken to her in . . . it must be a decade now."

"I know that. You probably haven't heard that she . . ."

"Wait a second. Slow down. This is pretty weird for me. You popping up out of nowhere like this. I told you I haven't seen or spoken to Abby since before the war."

"David, I'm sorry to call up out of the blue like this. Please hear me out. The reason I wanted to get in touch is, well, you may not have heard about Abby's illness . . ."

"I don't know anything about it."

"She was finding it harder and harder to swallow. They diagnosed a tumor in her trachea. About three months ago. She had an operation to have it removed."

"I'm sorry to hear that. I really am. But Abby and I lost touch a long, long time ago. The parting wasn't exactly friendly. You, of all people, should know that."

"I do, David. I thought you'd still want to be told, though. Things took a turn for the worse last week. She passed away early Wednesday morning."

"Good God."

"Just wanted to let you know what'd happened. Fill you in on the funeral arrangements. In case you wanted to attend. I found your number in the book. I wanted to check I had the right person, right address . . ."

"Sure, sure. Look . . . sorry I was so prickly."

"Forget it. I understand."

"Did she . . . um . . ."

"It was peaceful, David. There were some hard times. But in the end she passed away in her sleep. I was there, her mother was there. It was all very peaceful."

"Good. I mean . . . it's such a shock. I didn't even know she was ill."

"Sorry to give it to you like that.. I just thought that, in spite of everything, you'd probably want to know."

"I appreciate that.. Not an easy call to make."

"I'll send a card with the funeral details. It's next Tuesday."

"Okay. I'd like to go."

"Guess I'll see you there, then."

"Guess so. Jeff . . . I'm awfully sorry to hear this. I really am. My condolences. Thanks for calling."

•

I'd been leaning forward, all tensed up and sweating; now I fell back in my chair. For a while I sat there, gazing at the painting on the wall opposite my desk. I picked up the phone again: "Miss Stearn, I'm not feeling so well. Could you please cancel Mr. Stone this afternoon? Maybe fit him in next Tuesday. I think I have a free hour then."

"Yes, Doctor. Anything I can do for you?"

"No no. Just a little off-color, that's all. Think I'll go home and lie down for a bit. I'll look in at the end of the day."

I grabbed my hat and coat, and as I crossed the waiting room, my secretary threw me a peculiar look, almost of horror. I was on the verge of saying something else, but surprised by her expression, I looked away and made my way to the door. I walked down the five flights of stairs to the lobby—not so much for the exercise, more to avoid the elevator operator. He always tried to engage me in small talk, usually on something I knew nothing about, like baseball or movie gossip. I wasn't in the mood for it.

I was going to hail a cab back to my apartment. I stood at the curb, but then changed my mind and started aimlessly wending through the midafternoon throng. It wasn't particularly cold out, but the air was crisp. Long fingers of creamy light slipped between the buildings, slanting their way across Park Avenue. Gigantic cloud formations clotted the sky. I walked on, block after block. It was the first time in years that I'd simply wandered the streets on a weekday, without purpose. In a daze, as if I'd just been fired or something.

Many blocks on, I pulled out of my introspection and looked up. I was somewhere in the East Fifties, not far from my apartment. I remembered a nearby café-bar where Abby and I used to meet up. Run by a Frenchman, it had a long zinc bar top and had felt like a Paris café—or at least our idea of

one. We'd probably thought we were the height of sophistica-
tion drinking there.

Although I lived close by, I hadn't walked down this street
since Abby had left. Strange to see how little had changed.
There was the jeweler's store where I'd once bought Abby a
necklace. Opposite, a man was hawking the afternoon papers,
next to a cobbler bent over his work. Exactly as I'd left them,
as if they'd only just snapped back into action. And yet when
I came to where the French café used to be, it had vanished.
In its place was an anonymous-looking bar and grill, such as
you might find anywhere in the city.

Simply walking through its doors sent a chill of alienation
through me—everything inside felt simultaneously familiar
and strange. The zinc bar top had been ripped out and replaced with a bland, laminated counter. Chairs, tables, and
decor had all been replaced; the clientele was different. I'd
thought Abby and I had first talked about getting married
here, but now I wasn't so sure.

"What'll it be?"

"Give me a beer."

As a rule I never drank during the day, but I downed the
beer the bartender put before me and quickly ordered another. I gazed through the glass front into the streetscape,
washed in the somber colors of a fall afternoon.

As I drank, my thoughts drifted back. I was remembering my
freshman year at Columbia, it must have been 1936. That second semester, when I'd joined a college theater group, out of
sheer loneliness. One day in the rehearsal room, I'd felt someone watching me, and had looked up. Abby. I could still feel
the erotic jolt, so disturbing now that I knew she was dead. I'd
met her gaze and then let my eyes run down her body, taking

in her hips and breasts under the flimsy stage gown. A few minutes later, she'd left in the company of a short, intense-looking man, years older than me. I'd made enquiries the next day, and discovered who she was. A Barnard girl. A fine arts undergraduate who wanted to be an actress, and who apparently had the talent for it too.

Months had gone by. We'd attended rehearsals together. We'd even been in a play together—her in a leading role, me with a bit part. But we'd barely exchanged a dozen words. Then came a production of *The Winter's Tale*. Someone had pulled out at the last minute, and I'd landed a more substantial part this time around, much of it in dialogue with Abby. We'd had two weeks of rehearsal for a six-night run. But as opening night had drawn nearer, I'd felt increasingly ill at ease and out of my depth. Abby had suggested we go through our scenes on our own, away from the rest of the cast. She'd been sharing a room in a college dorm: that was where we'd practiced, while her roommate was in class. And that was where everything had started, on two narrow beds hastily pushed together.

I remembered being on stage not long after that, for the third or fourth performance of *The Winter's Tale*. The nerves had finally gone and the words had flowed effortlessly. I'd felt the magic of becoming someone else, if only for an hour or two. Afterward there'd been drinks, and then later Abby had smuggled me into her dorm through the laundry window, her roommate conveniently away for the weekend. An entire night had stretched out before us, when all we'd had before was the odd snatched moment. It had felt like the greatest luxury to watch Abby as she'd undressed without hurry. I could see her vividly now. My hand on her breast, her hand on my hand, her mouth to my ear, a line from the play that had become a secret code. Everything seemed to resolve to this frozen moment of expectation.

How to grieve for someone you haven't seen in over a decade? It felt absurd. But in a way, Abby had never entirely disappeared. Every now and then I'd catch her looking out from a billboard or a newspaper ad for some Broadway show. She'd never become a star or gone to Hollywood—her face wasn't right—but she'd managed to carve out a career in the theater nonetheless. It had only been a year ago that I'd last looked up to see her image on a poster outside the Century, for a show she was in with the Lunts. The poster had stayed up a couple of months, and I must have walked past it a good half-dozen times. I remembered thinking she'd aged a bit in the past few years, but perhaps she was already ill then. Before her death, weeks might go by without my giving her a single thought—and yet I'd known she was there, still watching over me. Now, I could feel myself fragmenting without the glue of that gaze.

I looked up from my glass. Only a few others were in the bar, most of them sitting by themselves. It was foreign to me, this world where you idled away your weekday afternoons drinking. The man to my left perched uncertainly on a stool nursing a whiskey, talking to an imaginary companion. Even if he hadn't been mumbling, I could tell from his eyes that he was in the grip of delusion; I'd seen it so often before. His scarred face even reminded me of a former patient, one of my earliest. A curious fellow who, years after I'd stopped seeing him, had developed the delusion that he was really a psychiatrist, by the name of Dr. David Manne, with an office on Park Avenue. It must have been a convincing performance, because every now and then some perplexed nurse or doctor would call me up to check the story.

Eventually a trickle of office workers started to come into the bar, just ahead of rush hour. The two worlds—that of the drifters and that of the workers—momentarily overlapped. I drank up, paid up, and wandered onto the street with no clear agenda. The thought of going home filled me with anguish. It was, after all, the same one-bedroom walk-up that Abby and I had briefly shared after we'd married. I'd stayed put after she'd left, and was somehow still there, a decade later. The rent was so cheap, I'd always reasoned, that it was the only way I could afford my expensive office. But as I made my way up Sixth Avenue, I knew that something had shifted inside me, that I'd never again feel comfortable in my apartment. I was finished with it.

Passing by a phone booth I stopped for a moment. I felt a compulsion to call up Jeff Speelman, to apologize again for my rudeness, to quiz him about Abby's life of the past ten years, of which I knew virtually nothing. The solitary existence I'd been leading meant that, if not for Speelman, I might never have found out about her death. The thought shocked me. For a long time after Abby had left me for him, I'd nurtured a corrosive bitterness toward Speelman. Now I felt almost grateful. Of course, I couldn't phone him since I didn't know his number. And I wondered how he'd gotten mine. He'd told me he'd looked me up in the phone book, but that had been a blatant lie. Both my office and home numbers were unlisted.

A tide of people flowed onto the sidewalks now as rush hour suddenly picked up and I found myself surrounded, alone. For a minute or two a young couple—early twenties— were walking beside me, and then just in front of me. I couldn't hear what they were saying, but the dynamic was clear: the man handsome yet timid, unsure of himself; the woman beautiful and outgoing, a little older, the dominant one. I had the impression of watching myself and Abby, as we were a decade ago, just before she'd left me. I even fought an urge to approach the couple, as if to warn them of what was in store. A sensation of the unreality of the city and its people hit me. Momentarily, the world felt like nothing more than a collective illusion.

I'd been heading toward Central Park without realizing it. Now I wandered through its gates. Without consciously intending to, I ended up sitting by the stone bridge over the Pond, watching the geese as they glided effortlessly across the water. The sky had cleared; the sun sat low in the sky. The scene before me was like a stage set for my epiphany after the shock of Abby's death. I was waiting for some sort of catharsis, but nothing came.

As I sat there, I forced myself to mentally step back, take stock of things. My ex-wife had just died. Since the end of my marriage, I'd been living in a kind of stasis. Yes, there'd been girlfriends, love affairs, although not recently, and never for long. They'd occasionally disturbed a life that inevitably drifted back to its point of equilibrium. As for my career, I'd worked hard for my degree, but had then chosen to work outside the medical hierarchy, setting up on my own. I'd ended up in psychiatry, a peculiarly unsatisfactory field, where patients rarely became better and often became worse. I worked on papers that were usually turned down by the medical journals for being too "speculative." After the failure of my marriage, I'd waited for the moment when the pieces would fit together, when I'd know what to make of my life and how to go on. Somehow, that moment had never arrived.

2

On the way back to my office, I couldn't shake the feeling that someone was following me. I'd had it earlier in the day as well, but had been too absorbed in my thoughts to let it distract me. Objectively, medically, I could put it down to the mild paranoia that sometimes accompanies shock, although that didn't make the feeling any less real. I even caught myself looking over my shoulder at one point, just to be sure. And as I did, I thought I glimpsed a man dive into a doorway, as if to hide. I almost went back to investigate, before telling myself I was being ridiculous.

Rush hour was winding down. I didn't even know why I was returning to my office, since my secretary would have left by now. In the elevator up, the operator was uncharacteristically silent. He stared at me until I caught his eye and he glanced away awkwardly. Perhaps I looked disheveled or something, after my afternoon's drinking, my long ramble across Manhattan. Here, in this well-heeled Park Avenue building—plush doctors' rooms on the lower floors, opulent apartments above—I was an impostor. There'd been a time, years ago, when I'd thought the address would help my career. Now I was wondering why I still kept up the facade, which I could barely afford by skimping on everything else. Somewhere downtown would cost four times less, and serve just as well. Not only was I done with my apartment, I realized, I was done with my office as well.

I was at my office door again, momentarily transfixed by a tiny brown mark underneath the doorknob. It had been there for years, surviving the weekly attentions of cleaning ladies and even a repainting last spring. I turned the doorknob and was surprised to find the door unlocked. Inside, evening rays filtered through the Venetian blind, illuminating the dust particles. In the gray twilight, the room gave me a similar sensation to the bar I'd been in—a disorientating blend of familiarity and strangeness.

"Hello, David."

I'd been looking toward the receptionist's desk; now I spun around. A man was sitting in the waiting area, deep in the shadows.

"Good God. You gave me a shock. What are you doing here?"

"Got a job for you. Afraid it can't wait. Your secretary let me in. Gave me the keys when she left. Told me to give them back to the doorman if you didn't show up."

"You pick your moments. I'm dead tired. What's it about? Where is it?"

"Not far. Don't worry, it won't take long."

"Seriously. I've had a hell of a day. Can't you find someone else?"

"David. Please. I promise, it won't take long."

"Why are you sitting in the dark?"

I snapped the light on. D'Angelo was fidgeting with the

police cap in his lap. The top button of his uniform was undone as if it were too hot in the room.

"All right then. Fill me in."

"Guy in his thirties. A veteran. Hasn't worked since he came back. He was having some kind of psychotic turn. His wife called us in. She's a little beat up. I've got a car outside. Just let me call the station, see if they've taken him in, or whether he's still at the apartment."

It was my sideline work. I was on call for incidents like this, when the police needed a psychiatrist's signature to get someone temporarily committed. In return, I was paid a monthly retainer. Not strenuous work; not pleasant either. But it was money I needed, and no matter how tired I was, I didn't want to rebuff D'Angelo. In any case, it was an excuse to delay facing my own apartment.

Minutes later we were in his police car. For a moment, as we swept down the dark avenue, I thought of telling D'Angelo about Abby. I had this idea it would give me some perspective, make Abby's death feel more real. But D'Angelo seemed preoccupied, disinclined to talk. For form's sake, I asked after his wife Maureen, then stumbled when I couldn't remember the name of his kid. Small talk stuttered to a halt.

In the silence—punctuated by the staccato of the police radio—I thought about D'Angelo. We'd been in high school out on the Island together, and for a while we'd been close. We'd both hovered on the edge of the same social group, without ever plunging in: that was how we'd found each other, as two outsiders. The following few months we'd been inseparable. And yet, under the surface, we'd had little in common. My interests had been cerebral; his more practical. I'd wanted to go to college; he hadn't. I'd been brought up alone by an uncle and aunt, to whom I was not particularly close; he'd been raised in a tight-knit family with many siblings. After high school we'd inevitably drifted apart, but through a series of chance encounters had just about kept in touch. Once, Abby and I had bumped into him in the Park, and he'd joined our picnic. Another time, we'd arranged to meet for a drink in a midtown bar. But it had been a strained affair, full of awkward silences and forced laughter, and after that, I hadn't really expected to hear from him again.

Then one morning D'Angelo had turned up at my office, unwashed and unkempt. It had been just as I was starting out, not long after Abby had left me. I'd had to keep him waiting, as I'd had patients until lunch. When I was finally free, I'd taken him down to a coffee place behind the avenue. He'd spun me a sob story, then hit me for a loan. We'd walked to my bank nearby; I'd withdrawn a generous sum for him. When I'd handed over the money, he'd broken down crying. "Please, please," I'd pleaded. I didn't care about the money, even if I could hardly afford it, but I couldn't take a scene. Perhaps he'd realized that: he'd straightened up, shaken my hand, and strode off. About six months later, he'd sent me a check in the mail. I never banked it, though; I hadn't wanted any further embarrassment in case it bounced.

Years after that episode, I'd received a call from him. He'd changed, utterly. He'd gotten himself back on track; he was a police officer now. On the phone he'd sounded assured, businesslike. He needed a psychiatrist to advise on the mental state of a man they'd detained. The usual police doctor wasn't available, could I step in? And so he'd put me onto this sideline work. Our relationship had been placed on a professional footing, which somehow allowed us to be easy with each other again. The incident of the loan and the uncashed check had never come up, and I doubted it ever would. It was a silent bond between us, of undetermined importance. Sitting in the car beside him now, watching him as he drove, it occurred to me that there was, after all, one thing we had in common. Although we didn't look alike, we both had evenly featured, everyman kind of faces. The sort that could simply dissolve into a street crowd.

The blocks flashed by in a streetlight blur. I thought about the job at hand. I'd been involved in dozens of these on-the-spot committals, but this wasn't the way they usually worked. Normally, D'Angelo or another officer would phone, and I'd go down to the station. I'd examine the detained person, if possible, and ask a few questions. Then I'd give an opinion, sign the papers. If I was busy, I'd always assumed other doctors were on call. D'Angelo had never before turned up out of the blue at my office.

"It's here."

We pulled into a poorly lit downtown street I didn't recognize, and parked on a corner. Rows of tenements stretched out endlessly into the blackness. Crossing the street, we made our way up the garbage-strewn stairway of a rundown building to a third-floor apartment, its front door slightly ajar. Inside, a room with peeling walls, a table and two chairs, a sofa, a formulaic painting of a seaside scene hanging opposite a tiny window. It felt like a hurried approximation of a living room, rather than an actual one. On one of the chairs sat a stocky, square-jawed man, thirties, plain dark suit, coolly smoking, legs splayed defiantly. A young woman leaned against the wall, the bare lightbulb above bleaching the color out of her face.

"Mrs. Esterhazy, this is Dr. Manne. He's going to talk to your husband."

She looked up wordlessly. Her cotton floral dress—lightweight for the season—had a small tear across the shoulder; there was a dark mark under her left eye. The man in the chair said: "Speak to him. Say hello."

"Good evening, Doctor."

I nodded, turned to D'Angelo: "This is the man?"

"No no. This is Mr. . . . . He's a family friend. The man you need to see is through there."

A door in the far wall opened onto an identically sized room, with only a chair, a mattress, and various bits of debris scattered over the floor. A man was lying on the mattress, rail thin, eyes half closed, thick hair plastered down with sweat. D'Angelo's young partner, Franklin, was watching over him: "He's calmed down now. Kinda drifting off I think."

"Okay, give me the story."

"We got the call and came down. This man, Esterhazy, was ranting away, all agitated. He had that broken bottle in his hand." Franklin pointed to where it lay in the corner of the room. "He'd taken a swing at his wife . . ."

"Did you see that?"

"No. It's what she said. Anyway, we restrained him. He eventually quieted down. Officer D'Angelo went out to find you."

"You've been here all this time? You didn't take him down to the station? Why do you think he's a psychiatric case?"

"Well . . ."

D'Angelo, who had followed me through, now interrupted: "He was rambling and ranting, talking about people out to get him, he was seeing things. The whole paranoid act."

"Had he been drinking?"

"According to his wife, he doesn't drink."

I crouched down: "Mr. Esterhazy, can I talk to you? Open your eyes, please. How many people can you see in the room, Mr. Esterhazy? Can you tell me?"

Franklin and I sat him up. He was staring at the wall, pupils dilated, a puzzled look on his face. A wave of tiredness hit me. I was having difficulty concentrating; everything seemed bathed in a gray, unreal light. I rubbed my eyes, tried to shake it off. Eventually, the feeling passed. I kept talking to Esterhazy, until he snapped out of his daze. Now he looked frightened, vulnerable: "Who are you? What do you want from me?"

"It's all right. My name is Dr. Manne. I'm here to help you."

"I . . . I want to talk to you alone."

"These are police officers. You can talk in front of them."

"No. They're trying to put me in the madhouse. They're saying I'm insane. I'm not insane."

"Nobody's saying anything. We're just trying to work out what happened. These officers tell me you threatened them with a broken bottle. And you hit your wife. Is that true?"

Esterhazy laughed uncertainly. "This is crazy. I don't have a wife. My wife is dead. We split up a long time ago. They're trying to . . ."

"Have you been drinking?"

"No. They drugged me. It's made me lose my . . . I'm confused. They're trying to put me away."

"Who drugged you?"

"Ask *them* . . ." He gesticulated at D'Angelo and Franklin. D'Angelo looked at me and shrugged. I checked for needle marks on the man's arm, but couldn't see any.

"Why would anyone drug you?"

But Esterhazy was drifting off again: "It's all mixed up . . . I've been brought here against my will . . ."

Under my breath, I said to D'Angelo: "Bring his wife in."

I'd been at dozens of scenes like this. There was no commoner delusion than that the police, or the doctor, or the wife, or the family was trying to get the subject committed for nefarious reasons. The fear and confusion: they, too, were typical. And yet something didn't feel right. But what with the tiredness, and the events of the day, I was no longer confident of my own reactions. I glanced over to the bottle in the corner, its bottom neatly shorn off. I looked about for the bottom, or its shattered remains, but couldn't see a single shard of glass.

Esterhazy's wife had come into the room now. She looked away as I turned my attention toward her: "Here, let me see your cheek."

"No, no, it's all right."

"Well . . . I'd go see a doctor in the morning. Check nothing's broken."

I hadn't wanted to examine the bruise so much as get a better look at her face. It was hard to place: she was young, but that might have meant anywhere between eighteen and thirty. Her good looks, trim figure, tightly coiffed hair—it all had a flat, generic quality to it.

"Mr. Esterhazy, are you saying that this is not your wife?"

"What did you just call me? That's not my name. And no, she's not my wife. Never seen her before today."

"Darling, don't be ridiculous."

"Don't call me that." He looked at her blankly. "I'm telling you, I've never seen her before today. I don't know what's happening to me. I'm here against my will. They've drugged me."

"What year is it, Mr. Esterhazy?"

"I told you, that's not my name. It's Smith."

"What year is it?"

"1949."

"What month?"

"September."

"What day?"

"Friday . . . I think."

"All right."

I signaled to Franklin to sit Esterhazy down again, while I ushered D'Angelo and Esterhazy's wife back through to the other room. The square-jawed man I'd originally mistaken for Esterhazy was still sitting there in his dark suit, smoking. I couldn't help but feel threatened by his presence, his silence.

The wife started whimpering. "I'm very sorry, Doctor. I don't know what's wrong, I don't know why he won't recognize me. It's horrible. Of course, I can show you photos . . ."

"That won't be necessary, Mrs. Esterhazy. Just tell me in your own words what happened."

She took a moment to pull herself together. "He came home. He was acting strange. He came into the kitchen while I was cooking. He put his arms around my waist. He was talking about some plot against him or something. He started threatening me. Then he hit me . . ."

Was it a New York accent? Surely not from these parts, anyway, not from the tenements. Like her face, her voice seemed neutral, unplaceable. She talked on tearfully for another minute or so, but I was hardly listening. I noticed how she kept looking over to the square-jawed man, as if silently asking for his approval. For a moment, I wondered whether they were lovers. Psychosis rarely comes out of nowhere; usually there's some sort of trigger. Perhaps Esterhazy had discovered the affair; perhaps that was the trigger . . . It was pointless speculation, I knew—I was drifting away from the facts.

The woman had stopped talking. D'Angelo pushed some forms across the table for me to sign and I took out my pen. As I went to sign, I felt some vague affinity with Esterhazy. As if his confusion were in some way mine as well.

"Where are you taking him?"

"Um. Stevens Institute."

"Stevens Institute?" The name meant something to me, but I couldn't pin down where I'd heard it. "Why not City Psychiatric?"

"Don't ask me. That's what I was told at the station. Stevens Institute."

I scribbled a note and signature at the bottom of the forms. "I'm signing him in for forty-eight hours. If they want to keep him longer, the doctor in charge will have to send me a report first."

Minutes later, I stood across the road from the building, keeping well within the shadows. I'd refused D'Angelo's offer of a lift home—for some reason I'd wanted to watch unobserved as he and Esterhazy came out of the building. But after a good quarter of an hour, there was still no movement. Another wave of tiredness hit me. In a way I was glad of it; I'd be knocked out as soon as I got home, too exhausted to be spooked by my own apartment.

The occasional figure haunted the sidewalk, but it felt preternaturally quiet for Manhattan. I was somewhere on the Lower East Side, a couple of blocks from the water. In the other direction, the shabby street I was on crossed an avenue. I made my way toward it, flagged down a cab.

"Where to, Mac?"

"East Fifty-Sixth, corner of First."

The driver turned back down where I'd come from and soon we were speeding through an industrial wasteland by the river, its derelict buildings gaping like teeth. I looked at my watch, and was surprised to find that it was not even nine o'clock.

"Going out or going home?"

"Home."

"Lucky you. Me, I'm on all night." Silence for a minute or two, then the driver continued: "Trouble is, you never know what the wife's up to when you work all night, do you? I call her up. Stop the cab, go to a phone booth. Sometimes at one or two in the morning. Nine times out of ten she doesn't answer. Says she's in bed, doesn't want to get up. But what do I know?"

I couldn't tell whether it had been a bit of banter or something else, so I made an indistinct noise by way of reply. The driver lapsed into silence again, and a tension reigned in the cab. I found myself thinking about Esterhazy's wife, visualizing her. The bruise on the cheek, almost too vivid, but no obvious swelling. The slightly robotic way she'd talked, despite the tears. The barely noticeable twitch in her leg, betraying trauma—or perhaps nervousness. I gazed through the window into a mist of drizzle. Then what seemed like moments later, the cab pulled into the curb. I was outside my building again. It was as if an eternity had passed since I'd last been there.

Through the iron gates and up two flights of stairs. My front door opened onto a corridor and a small kitchen. An archway led through to the living room, which looked out over a courtyard, and because the building opposite had no windows, it felt very private. A tiny refuge in the vastness of the city. The bedroom was hardly bigger than the double bed, over which hung a painting of a nude that Abby had left there. That was it, as far as decorations went. I hadn't felt like homemaking after Abby had gone, and then after a while I'd grown to prefer the starkness. A girlfriend I'd once invited over had been shocked by this emptiness—as if I'd only just moved in, although I'd been there years. On these rare occasions when someone visited I realized what a strange place it was for a Park Avenue doctor to end up in. That, in turn, discouraged me from inviting people over.

I looked about the living room. Everything different, everything the same. I remembered how soul destroying it had been, in those first weeks after Abby had gone, to be forever coming back home to find everything exactly as I'd left it.

Around the small table were two chairs, the same design but each slightly different. Abby had always sat in one particular chair and I in the other. Even now, ten years on, I used the same one and left the other empty. Similarly with the bed: I always slept on the same side. Once a year or so, I'd have a powerfully erotic dream about Abby—I hoped to God that was finished with now. Eventually I found a couple of sleeping pills in the kitchen cupboard, and chased them down with some whiskey from a dusty bottle I hadn't touched in months. Even if I was dead tired, I wanted to be sure.

3

Saturday morning. I lay in bed an hour longer that usual, feeling neither tired nor well rested, wondering what to do with the day. If my workweek was tightly scheduled, weekends were generally free-form—in theory at least. Actually, it occurred to me now, they were no less scripted than my professional life. The day would start with breakfast over the *Times*, always at the same diner on the corner. In the afternoon I'd go to the Park with a novel, if it was fine, or visit a gallery, if it wasn't. Occasionally I'd have an evening engagement; otherwise I'd go to the movies, or listen to music at home. And that was how it always went. The thought of doing it all over again today and tomorrow—and then next weekend and the one after—filled me with a sense of futility. The weekend routine: that too, it now seemed, was over.

My thoughts kept circling around Esterhazy and his wife, picking over little details from the night before. D'Angelo appearing at my office. The open door of the apartment. The too-neat, almost coquettish rip in the woman's dress. The

broken bottle, with no broken glass. A half-dozen other in-
congruities. The more I brooded, the odder the events of the
evening seemed. I continued in this vein for a while, dreaming up hypotheses, before finally pulling myself out of it. I was
overthinking things again. If I drew back a little, broadened
my perspective, I could see that nothing about last night was
as strange as all that. I recognized within me that desire to
enter into the patient's fantasy, and resisted it. If I were leading the life of a normal man, I reasoned, I wouldn't be fretting
over minutiae like this. I'd simply be getting on with things.
Taking my son to the game, perhaps. Or a date out to lunch.
Or playing a round of golf with an old college buddy. And yet,
that wasn't the whole of it either. That wasn't the only reason I
was creating these complications for myself. There was Abby.
I was using the Esterhazy case to avoid thinking about her.

Finally I got out of bed. I was ravenously hungry; with everything that had happened yesterday, I'd skipped dinner. As
I shaved, I stared at my face in the mirror with more curiosity
than usual. For a moment or two, under the intensity of my
own gaze, it began to look strange. As if, instead, I were staring at a wax model of myself. It was that same sensation of the
unreality of things that had struck me the day before, wandering around Manhattan. But then, in a blink, everything
was normal again. The face was mine.

It was still fairly early, but the street was already mobbed
with Saturday shoppers. Stopping outside the diner where I
ritually had my breakfast, I felt like an actor hitting his spots.
I ordered the same thing every morning, yet each time the
waitress would make a point of giving me a menu before taking my order. An awkward charade, but it had always been
like that and could never now be different. I'd never developed
the kind of bantering, flirtatious relationship that the waitress had with several other male customers. I peered inside,

without entering. There she was, chatting to another regular. I must have seen him in there hundreds of times. I even knew quite a bit about him, from overheard conversations. I knew that he lived on Sutton Place, just around the corner from my apartment. I knew that he worked in insurance, that he had a son, and that his son was blond-haired. I knew that he was separated from his wife, who lived somewhere in Brooklyn. I knew a dozen other facts—trivial or otherwise—without ever having exchanged a word with him. I wondered how I'd spent so many hours in that diner.

A few blocks later, I grabbed a couple of hot dogs from a street vendor and wolfed them down as I walked along, unsure of where I was going or what I was doing. I picked up a copy of the *Times*, then found myself drifting down into the subway on Fifty-Seventh, boarding a train heading downtown. It, too, was full of Saturday shoppers, but I managed to find a seat and leafed through the newspaper. The front page was given over to Truman's announcement that the Russians had detonated an atom bomb. Inside, a morbid opinion piece said that lower Manhattan, with its tall buildings crammed into such a small area, was now a perfect target. I turned to the back of the paper, and scanned down the list of names in the obituary column. Seeing her name in black and white might have changed things, but there was no mention of Abby.

I'd had a half-formed plan to go down to the Village, but when I finally looked up from the paper, I realized I'd missed the stop. Eventually I got off at East Broadway. Not a neighborhood I knew, but as soon as I emerged onto the street, I realized why I'd ended up there. It was near where I'd been last night. God knows why I was retracing my steps, but that was what I seemed to be doing.

I walked down to Manhattan Bridge to orient myself. Then

after an hour or so of wandering about, I found Esterhazy's
street. At first, I wasn't sure I had the right place. It was bustling
and animated, filled with stalls and street peddlers, whereas
last night it had been deserted, sinister—another feeling altogether. It puzzled me, but finding Esterhazy's building settled
the question. The broken stair on the stoop: I'd almost fallen
over it the night before. And there it was again.

I hung about opposite, smoking a cigarette, at a loss as to
what I was doing there. I was watching Esterhazy's building,
but I was thinking about Abby. Just as at home, in the apartment I'd briefly shared with Abby, I'd been thinking about
Esterhazy. What shook me was the thought that in all these
years, I could have simply picked up the phone and asked her
to meet me for a drink. She'd have said yes, I was sure of it.
I could imagine it so easily now. The initial surprise in her
voice when she picks up my call. The coolness. Then finally a
cautious agreement to meet me for an hour, no more, somewhere on the Upper West Side where she lived. We meet. It's
awkward. But once she understands that I'm calm, that I don't
want anything from her, we both relax a bit. Talk about our
lives. She shows some interest in my work. Says she'll send me
tickets to her current show. I shake my head, say: "It's nice of
you to offer, but . . ." and then before I know it, the hour is up.
After the first few difficult minutes, it had gone by so quickly.
"I have to go now," she says. We get out of our booth. Outside
the bar, we stand looking at each other for a long moment.
Finally I say, "I'm glad you came. Give my regards to Jeff."
She nods, says: "I'm glad I came too." I say: "I'll always want
the best for you." She nods, kisses me on the cheek, and that's
that. I won't see her again, not ever again, unless by accident.
But I'll be able to go on. I'll no longer be stuck in this state of
suspension.

I stood there on the street corner, lost in my fantasy, almost

in tears. Missed opportunities: they were so peculiarly deso-
lating. Even if I'd phoned her and she'd rebuffed me, I could
have written her a note. Saying that I wanted nothing from
her, only the best for her. And even if she hadn't responded
to that, I could have been secure in the knowledge that at
least she'd read it. Instead, our last contacts dated back to the
months after her departure, when I'd behaved abominably.
Pestering her, stalking her, calling her up at ridiculous hours
of the night . . . the thought was too much to bear. Then there
was Speelman. Yesterday I'd felt grateful toward him. Now I
felt angry. Why had he waited until it was too late? Why hadn't
he given me an opportunity to make my peace with her?

Out of the corner of my eye, I saw a couple of men come
out of Esterhazy's building. One of them well groomed, elegantly dressed, quite out of place given the surroundings. The
other was the square-jawed man from last night, I was almost
certain, the one who'd sat at the table smoking. I noticed that
he was still in his dark suit of the night before, and that settled
it in my mind. The two of them turned north, walking at a
fair pace in the direction of Chinatown. Without thinking,
I tossed my cigarette into the gutter and set off after them.
They were in deep conversation, and the smooth-looking one
was wagging his finger at the square-jawed one, but whether
he was doing it aggressively or simply to illustrate a point, I
couldn't tell. Within seconds of seeing them, I was inventing little scenarios as to what they were up to, what the relationship between the two might be. The adrenaline flushed
through my body as they rounded a corner, and I quickened
my pace.

A minute or so later, it was all over. By the time I'd turned
the corner, they were nowhere to be seen. I sprinted ahead,
scanning the sidewalks. Had they seen me? Gone into another
building? Gotten into a car? I was flummoxed, furious with

myself. I couldn't believe how quickly I'd managed to lose them. I hung about feeling stupid, then slowly made my way back to Esterhazy's road—my heart still hammering against my ribcage, my thoughts racing. I replayed in my mind the scene of the two men leaving Esterhazy's building. Had one of them hesitated over the broken step? I thought he had, but perhaps even this early on, only minutes after the event, I was already elaborating on my memories.

I thought about Esterhazy's wife. Would she be alone in the apartment now? If I wanted to see her, I just about had a legitimate excuse. After all, even if her husband was now under some other doctor's charge, he was ultimately my responsibility, since I'd signed his papers. It didn't make much sense, but I crossed the street anyway, then strode up the three flights of stairs.

No answer. I knocked again. Not a sound. I'd guessed there'd be no one there, but that didn't stop me from feeling deflated. After a minute or so, I bent down, stared through the keyhole. The same bare room I'd been in last night. A table with nothing on it. Two chairs. A bland picture on the wall. If anything, it looked even emptier in the daylight, so much so that I couldn't imagine anyone really living there. But what about my own apartment? It was hardly more furnished. I stood up, cocked my head toward the stairwell. Once again, this suspicion that I was being followed. Ridiculous. I'd heard a noise, but obviously it was somebody scraping about behind the door on the other side of the landing. I crossed over, knocked on the other door. I could hear labored breathing coming from the other side, but still no answer until I knocked again, harder.

"What d'you want?"

"I'm looking for Mrs. Esterhazy, from across the landing."

"Don't know nobody from across the landing."

"Mr. and Mrs. Esterhazy. They live on this floor."

"You mean the door opposite?"

"Yes."

"Ain't nobody lives there. Not permanent anyway. People come and go."

"What do you mean? Could you open the door so we can talk?"

"I mean ain't nobody lives there. Ain't opening the door to you or anyone else. Good day to you, mister."

At some point I had lunch at an automat, and then the afternoon was lost to another restless meander across Manhattan. Without my usual routine, I felt unmoored, drifting through the mass of anonymous bodies, wanting to be alone, yet lonely at the same time. As I turned a corner, a newspaper hawker was yelling out the headline: "Russians have the bomb!" I remembered that piece I'd read on the subway, about Manhattan's vulnerability to attack. Everything surrounding me—buildings, cars, people—could apparently now be vaporized in seconds. That simple fact seemed to steal some of the city's reality.

I rarely spent daytime hours in my apartment over the weekend—it was too claustrophobic—but sometimes I'd drop by my office to do paperwork. I considered doing that now, but could come up with no good reason for it. My mood kept jolting from numb sadness when thinking about Abby, to an excited unease when thinking about the Esterhazy case. Later, wandering around the Village, I passed by City Psychiatric, its neogothic gargoyles looming above me on Eleventh. How many people had I signed in to that hospital? How many had never left? I thought back to various occasions when the police had called me in for an opinion. Sometimes a single glance confirmed that a person was disturbed and dangerous. Other times, it was more borderline. Would I have had Esterhazy committed if I hadn't been so tired? If I hadn't felt some obscure pressure?

I'd finally realized something about Mrs. Esterhazy. Physically, she was very like one of my first patients, Miss Fregoli. The same bland good looks, young yet somehow ageless. And the same accent from nowhere. Miss Fregoli had suffered from a long-term melancholic illness, but after three months of therapy, I'd felt she'd made progress. The last time I'd seen her, she'd gone to a good deal of trouble over her appearance: new clothes, hairstyle, makeup. We'd discussed whether she should take a break from treatment. She'd seemed keen, and we'd agreed to suspend our twice-weekly appointments for a month. She'd been the last patient of my day and—unusually for me—I'd stopped for a drink on the way home, at a bar on Columbus Circle. It had been a private celebration of my success with Miss Fregoli, coming at a time when my self-esteem was low on account of Abby's recent departure. But a few days later, Miss Fregoli's mother had phoned me. Her daughter had hanged herself.

Hoping for some respite from my own mind, I ducked into a movie theater. When the mood struck, I could sit in the dark for hours on end, as one feature melded into the next, in a loop of endless narrative. The more generic the movie, the more absurd, the more removed from anything realistic or artistic, the more I liked it. I bought my ticket and settled down to watch a romantic picture with an even more ridiculous plot than usual: a showgirl falls in love with a returned war veteran suffering from amnesia. Characters flickered by in ghostly fashion—thoughts still circled me, just beyond my grasp, as if they were emanating from somewhere else. After an hour or so, well before the end of the movie, I stood up and wandered out into twilit streets.

I was thinking of Miss Fregoli again as I ordered my hamburger and coffee in a near-empty drugstore. In my mind's eye, her face had now merged with Mrs. Esterhazy's until they'd become indistinguishable. Miss Fregoli's death had been a huge blow. But it had also triggered my sporadic writing career, as she'd been the subject of my first paper. For months after her suicide, I'd tormented myself with the fact that she'd killed herself just when I'd thought she was improving. Then walking home from my office one evening, I'd had an idea. In the depths of depression, people cannot summon up the energy or courage for suicide. It's only when they get better that they can do it. The danger period is not when the depression is at its worst, I realized, but when the patient is pulling out of it. Throughout the night, I'd feverishly written up the case history and my conclusions. Journal after journal had turned the paper down, always finding it "interesting," but lacking the necessary "clinical rigor." Eventually, a small journal published by some Midwestern university had accepted the piece.

It was getting late when I finally returned home, but I wasn't tired. I felt dizzily on the verge of something, but I didn't know what. An odor of cigarettes was in the sitting room, although I rarely smoked at home, and hadn't for weeks. I picked up a coin from the table, flicked it into the air, caught it, then put it down again. Heads or tails? Abby and I had often played this game to decide what to what to do with our evenings. For the second night running, I poured myself a large whiskey, downed it, then poured myself another. By nature, I was an abstemious type—I'd drunk more in the past couple of days than I normally would in a month.

I eyed the gramophone in the corner of the room. Beside

it, the dozen or so records I owned. All Beethoven. All piano sonatas and string quartets. It was this music, more than
anything else, which filled the emotional space that had long
ago opened up within me. I took a record out of its sleeve,
dropped the needle onto it. The grooves were worn down
through overplaying now, although to my ears the accentu-
ated crackles only added further meaning, overlaying the
music with intimations of its own obsolescence. It sometimes felt as though the whole of a life had been lived within
those tolling tones of the slow movement of the "Appassio-
nata." Other music imposed a mood, but this soaked up one's
own mood, reached to the essence of it, and ultimately to the
end of it.

4

Again I lay in bed longer than usual. Feeling at a loose end, I flicked through my address book. D'Angelo's home number was there, although I couldn't recall his giving it to me. Even as I was dialing it I was wondering why—as though I were observing myself from a distance, with no access to my own motives. But once his wife had handed him the phone, I bluntly cut through the first few awkward exchanges.

"Something I didn't tell you the other day. If I seemed in a peculiar mood, it was because I'd had a bit of a shock. Remember my ex-wife?"

"Yeah. Abby, is it?"

"She died a few days ago. Cancer. I'd only just found out that afternoon."

"Ah. I'm sorry to hear that."

I could hear the slight hesitation. She wasn't my wife any more, after all, and it wasn't immediately clear whether condolences were due.

"It threw me, that's all. I'd had a few drinks. I'm concerned because I really shouldn't have gone to see Esterhazy. Wasn't in a fit state to give an opinion."

"Don't be ridiculous."

"I mean it, George."

"Listen. You sound like someone who could do with some company. It's going to be a fine day. Me and Maureen, we're going to set up the grill in the yard, cook some steak. Why don't you come over? We're in Howard Beach, not so far. Get the train from Penn Station. When you get in, call me and I'll pick you up."

A couple of hours later I was in D'Angelo's car. We were pulling into the drive of a neat, clapboard bungalow on a long, wide avenue of more-or-less identical clapboard bungalows. It had been so long since I'd been out of Manhattan that the quiet suburban streets felt like a foreign country. I hadn't been angling for an invitation, not consciously anyway, but had nonetheless jumped at D'Angelo's offer. After the past couple of days, I was surely in need of a perspective other than my own. And this felt like the kind of thing that people should be doing on a weekend. A family man invites an old friend over for a barbecue. What could be more normal than that? But on the train down, it started to seem less clear-cut. I wasn't really a friend of D'Angelo's, was I? Not since school, anyway. Why would he invite me over? It wasn't as if he'd ever done it before.

The weather had changed; the warm, hazy air felt more like August than late September. D'Angelo's wife was setting a table in the backyard. Although we'd only met once, she greeted me warmly with a kiss on the cheek. It was the first physical contact I'd had with a woman in months, and it sent a tiny shock through me. D'Angelo got us beers; their six-year-old boy was driving a toy truck across the lawn. The setup seemed so conventional, almost too ordinary, like some magazine advertisement portraying suburban life. I took a long gulp of cold beer that went right to my head—I'd skipped breakfast and was drinking on an empty stomach, I realized.

"Do you like comic books?"

Excited at having a guest for lunch, the boy had come and sat beside me while his parents got the meal ready.

"There weren't too many of them around when I was a kid. Do you like them?"

"Yes. My favorite character's The Shapemaker. Do you know The Shapemaker?"

"Afraid not."

"He's this man, his real name's Mike Brown, and one day he took some bad medicine, so now he can change shapes, and he has a friend who's a police officer like Dad, and sometimes he calls The Shapemaker, and The Shapemaker changes into other people, and helps him catch criminals . . ."

The boy's eyes shone with enthusiasm. We talked more about comic books then suddenly he jumped up and shouted: "Try and catch me!" We ran around the garden for a while until I brought him down with a playful tackle. Stimulated by the beer and physical exertion, I was invaded by a brief feeling of euphoria. Was this what it was like to have a wife, a child? I glanced at Maureen. She wasn't wildly attractive, but she had a nice, gentle face. She'd put on weight since I'd first met her, and I could see that she'd end up plump, but right now she had a beautifully voluptuous figure. It felt good to be walking to the table, holding hands with the boy, looking over to his smiling mother. For a moment, I was living in a parallel world—this was my house, my son, my wife, and we were about to have lunch outside on a sunny fall afternoon.

D'Angelo took me aside before we sat down. "There's

something inside I want to show you first." We went through to a spotless living room. A photo album sat on a coffee table. D'Angelo picked it up, flicked through it, took out a photograph. "Here, I found this." He handed it to me. A picnic scene: a young Abby staring straight out of the photo; me looking furtively to one side.

"Wherever did this come from?"

"Don't you remember that time you invited me to a picnic? In Central Park? I found it this morning. I want you to have it."

I nodded, shoved the photo into my pocket, and walked back out to the garden.

The steaks were good. An atmosphere of easy conviviality descended across the table as we chatted about everything and nothing. D'Angelo was in an expansive mood, talking about the boat he was going to buy for weekend outings. He put his hand on my back: "What the heck are you still doing in Manhattan? Why not get out? There's space here, there's air here. There's water. We can go for a swim after lunch. I'll lend you some trunks. Probably the last time this season." I nodded—the woozy sense of euphoria still lingered. Why indeed was I still in Manhattan? Why did life have to be so difficult, anguished? Surely it was all here. As simple as having lunch in the garden. Or watching a boy lying on the grass, laughing.

At one point Maureen turned to me: "George never told me how you two became friends."

"We were at school together. I don't really remember exactly how we . . ."

D'Angelo butted in: "David was the smart kid, the popular kid. I was the loner. Truth is I was being bullied. David stuck up for me and got the bullying stopped. No idea why he saw fit to befriend me, but thank God he did."

The response mystified me—that wasn't how things had

been—but I let it pass. After lunch, I helped wash the dishes, then D'Angelo and I drank some more beer and played a game of chess in the garden. It was hot, but cooling gusts of wind were coming in off the bay, shaking the already browning leaves onto the lawn. After the game, we sat out in deckchairs for a while, mostly in silence. But when I started talking about Esterhazy, I could sense D'Angelo stiffen, his face darken.

"Listen, David. We've worked together for a while, haven't we? It's been a couple of years now. You trust me, don't you?"

"'Course I do."

"Well, let me tell you. Esterhazy was damn crazy. He was swinging a broken bottle around and talking all kinds of crap. I've seen enough of those guys to know. Yeah, he'd calmed down by the time you turned up. Don't worry that you did anything wrong signing his papers. You didn't."

"I appreciate you saying that. You know I'm not supposed to rely on hearsay . . ."

D'Angelo cut me off: "Look, we may have some things to talk about, but this is not the right time."

"One last thing. Tell me about the Stevens Institute."

"I'll call you in the week, okay?"

"Sure."

We lapsed back into silence, but not the comfortable one of before. I could feel the photo D'Angelo had given me in my pocket. I remembered the picnic, but I didn't remember that picture being taken. Why would D'Angelo have had a camera with him anyway? I was pretty sure I hadn't invited him; we'd simply bumped into each other on the street or in the Park. Either he'd remembered it wrong, or I had. But what did it matter?

D'Angelo looked at his watch, not in a showy way, but I could tell it was a performance. "Gotta go soon, help a neighbor with some plastering and stuff. You could come . . ."

"No, it's been great, but I should be getting back."

"Okay. Well I'm glad you could make it out. Gotta come down again. Let me call you a cab."

No offer to drive me to the station. And the idea of the afternoon swim seemed to have gone out the window as well. D'Angelo went to phone, and I got up to say goodbye to the kid, who was playing on an old tire strung up to a tree to make a swing.

D'Angelo's wife came outside. "George tells me you have to go. What a shame. I'm really pleased you could come. It's so nice that George has a friend like you." She leaned over and kissed me on the cheek again. "Please come again. We're always around on weekends." As she spoke, she put her hand on my shoulder and rubbed it slightly, unmistakably.

5

On the train back I took out some work I'd brought, a rough draft of an article I'd wanted to read over. But I couldn't concentrate. Instead, I stared at the formless vista of suburbs and industry that slipped by as we trundled toward Manhattan. I'd lost confidence in my writing, I realized. It wasn't because of the difficulty in getting it published. No, the problem was that every time I came to a conclusion, explicitly stated an opinion, the opposite view would always start to look more attractive. And the paper would inevitably end up feeling like an elaborate fiction. Only my very first piece, on Miss Fregoli, had escaped this rule.

We pulled into Penn Station. The mill of people, even on a Sunday, was momentarily disorientating after the graveyard quiet of D'Angelo's suburb. I climbed the stairs to the main concourse with its gigantic clock, the second hand stuttering forward. One of my earliest memories was of this clock, on a trip from Long Island with my aunt and uncle, at the age of four or five. I gazed at the greenhouse roof high above as the late afternoon sunshine filtered in, spliced by the arched steel frame into a complicated game of light and shadow. I'd always found it comforting to arrive at this station. Its vastness, its Roman solidity. It had been there before I was born, was there as my memory had first been awoken, would be there long after I was dead.

I had that feeling again. That I was being followed, only it was more acute than before. Involuntarily I looked toward the Doric columns at the threshold of the waiting room. A man was standing there. He was wearing an ill-fitting suit and a fedora low over his forehead. I had the impression that I'd caught him looking away, although since a newspaper hid most of his face, how could I tell? But the conviction that this man was following me, and had been doing so for the past couple of days, seized me and wouldn't let go. I felt hived off into two different people—the one who knew absolutely that he was being followed, and the other who stood beside him, observing, rationalizing the feeling away.

I went into a phone booth and asked the operator to put me through to the Stevens Institute. Moments later a receptionist answered. I cooked up some story to make the receptionist to give me the address—it was somewhere way uptown. I hung up and glanced at the big clock again. It was nearly five.

The man hadn't moved. I went downstairs to the subway then waited around the corner by the ticket office, all the time telling myself how foolish I was being. When I'd all but given up I saw him again, coming down the same stairs. He was past me and through the turnstiles in a flash. It had all happened in such a whirl that once I'd gotten hold of myself again, it was probably too late to go after him. Or perhaps I didn't really want to. Still a side of me resisted ceding to this absurd notion that anyone was following me. How could he be, I reasoned, when he'd appeared a good five or six minutes after I'd gone down into the subway. By that time, normally, I might have already left the station.

I jumped on a crowded train. As it worked its way uptown, I reflected on the events of the day. Nothing was any clearer than it had been before lunch. Instead of giving me an outside perspective, seeing D'Angelo had plunged me deeper into myself. I remembered that brief moment of euphoria in the garden, willing myself to believe in D'Angelo's suburban idyll. I thought about his wife. No doubt she was bored out of her mind in Howard Beach. Bored with her husband coming home so late every evening, bored with their colorless existence. When she'd touched my shoulder, I'd felt a frisson and knew she'd felt it too. I imagined what it would be like to have an affair with her. The Manhattan assignations, the lunchtime cocktails. The afternoons at my apartment. Undressing her, laying her down on my bed. The desire. The cold, mechanical expulsion of it. I shook the idea from my mind.

The sky was a darkening gray. I was somewhere past Columbia. Very few people were around, and no one at all on the tree-lined street that the Stevens Institute was on. That was good, because at least I could now be certain that I wasn't being followed. I wondered why Esterhazy had been committed this far away; weren't there several downtown psychiatric hospitals? The Institute was a modest, anonymous-looking building. The one odd thing was that two military guards stood outside the main entrance—that threw me for a moment. I showed them my doctor's license and when one of them asked if I worked there, I took a chance and said yes. Through the doors I found myself in an atrium. A reception desk at one end was manned by a young man who I assumed was a medical student, earning a few extra bucks on a weekend.

"I've come to check on a patient I had committed here

two days ago. Here's my card. The patient's name is Peter Esterhazy."

The receptionist had me wait in an area just off the atrium.
I looked about, took in the details. Fresh paint, shiny carpet,
new chairs. The place had only just been opened or renovated,
and was a hell of a lot smarter than your average New York
psychiatric hospital. Nobody about, apart from the receptionist, when normally there was a constant to-and-fro in places
like these. As if to contradict my thoughts, a woman suddenly walked in from behind the receptionist's desk, crossed
the atrium, and went out the front door. For a bizarre moment I'd thought she was Abby, although on second glance
the resemblance was quite superficial. In the couple of days
since I'd learned of Abby's death, I'd already had this experience once or twice. I'd had it with former patients as well—
mistakenly thinking I'd seen them on the street. As though
actors from my past were continually coming back in different form.

"Dr. Manne? I'm afraid I can't get hold of the resident
doctor at the moment. He's probably gone to dinner. I'm not
really supposed to disturb him after six-thirty unless it's an
emergency. Is this an emergency?"

"No. But I'd like to see my patient."

"Well . . . the normal practice is to make an appointment
beforehand . . . perhaps I could fix a time for you to see Mr.
Esterhazy tomorrow?"

I was regretting saying it wasn't an emergency. I'd committed Esterhazy for forty-eight hours, and by tomorrow morning he'd either be gone, or no longer under my care.

"I appreciate that this is unusual, but I would like to exercise my right to see my patient. You can check Mr. Esterhazy's
records to verify that he was committed by me."

"I'll have to wait until I can get hold of the resident . . ."

I shook my head. "Under the committal procedures of this state, I have the right to see my patient when I wish. If you won't allow me that—right now—then I'm afraid I'll have to take your name and refer the matter to the authorities . . ."

I'd badly flustered him. I'd been doubly lucky to find the resident absent, and an inexperienced receptionist. He picked up the phone receiver and murmured into it. Within a minute a nurse had appeared. I signed a form and was then led down a long corridor to an elevator. As we walked, I continued to look around, astonished at how perfect everything seemed, when usually these places were so shabby. Surfaces had a high sheen. A sumptuous vase of flowers sat on a corner table— more Madison Avenue advertising agency than psychiatric ward. The nurse too was immaculately groomed, as if she'd just stepped out of a makeup department.

We rode the elevator, walked down another pristine corridor, and then the nurse said: "This is Mr. Esterhazy's room."

There was only one bed. The man lying on it was tall and wiry, with thick black hair. The man I'd committed had been tall and wiry, with thick black hair. And yet I wasn't sure, he looked different in some way. I was about to call in the nurse when he propped himself up and said: "Dr. Manne! Thank God you've come!"

I continued looking at him wordlessly. A chart was hanging off the end of his bed. I unhooked it. Marked at the top was "ESTERHAZY, PETER."

The man seemed perplexed by my silence. "Don't you know who I am? Downtown apartment. The woman there. Pretended to be my wife. Then they took me here."

"What's your name?"

"Smith. You remember me, don't you?"

A dizziness swept over me. I was staring into myself, full-length in a huge mirror hanging by the bed.

"They've drugged me. You've got to get me out of here, Doctor."

I squinted at the chart again. For a few seconds, the letters refused to form words. I shook my head and everything became clear again. The nurse had noted what he'd been given—heavy doses of sedatives. He'd spent the best part of the past two days under sedation, brought around for meals, then put under again.

"When was the last time they gave you pills?"

"Just before you came. You'll help me, won't you, Doctor?"

I could already see the sedatives taking effect—his voice slurring, the effort he was making to keep himself vaguely upright.

"Yes," I said finally. "I'll help you."

As I said those words, I realized that I was crossing a frontier. I was in a different world now, and there would be no easy way back.

Now I was in the back of a cab, with the man who had been released to me as Esterhazy. Somehow I'd gotten him up out of bed, into a bathrobe and slippers, down the elevator and along the corridor, with the nurse running behind me, arguing with me, telling me I couldn't do what I patently was in the middle of doing. Then I'd brazened it out with the receptionist—bullying, threatening, relying on the element of surprise, until finally he'd let me sign the release forms. I'd bundled the man into a cab that had passed moments after I'd heaved him through the front doors. It was a fantastic piece of luck that the resident had been out, and that there'd been no other senior doctor about, probably because it was a Sunday. Even then, I'd thought I'd seen the guards come after us, just as the cab had pulled from the curb.

"What's up with your friend?"

"Too much to drink, I'm afraid."

"Don't want no accidents in my cab."

"It'll be fine, don't worry."

The man had managed to stay conscious for the time it had taken me to get him out of the Institute. He'd kept murmuring: "You'll help me, won't you? You'll help me?" But now he was gently snoring. I'd gotten through it all on a rush of adrenaline; I was breathing deeply to slow down my heart rate, and even the brief conversation with the cabdriver had felt like a struggle. I peered out the window, taking in random fragments of the city as it flashed by—a broken fire hydrant, an old woman with a dog, a newspaper blowing down the avenue.

The cab slowed and stopped. I was about to ask the cabbie why, but then I noticed we were already outside my building. With great difficulty, I hauled the man up the two flights of stairs, as he fell in and out of consciousness. I unlocked the door. My apartment. There it all was again: chairs, table, books, gramophone records. The incredible strangeness of the overfamiliar. I got the man out of his things, put my pajamas on him, laid him down on my bed, and threw a blanket over him. I stared at his face, as if it were some sort of code I might decipher. But the more I stared, the more indecipherable it became. Nothing to do but let him sleep off the drugs. He could tell me his story tomorrow.

I sat at my small table. I poured myself the last of the whiskey. It had taken a year to drink half of the bottle, two days to drink the other half. I was hungry, but there was nothing to eat in the apartment. There never was; I ate every meal out. I didn't dare go get something; I didn't want to leave the man alone right now.

Thoughts bombarded me. Everything had changed, once

again. I'd no doubt lost my police work. What I'd done had
been unprofessional, if not downright illegal. I risked censure
from the Psychiatric Association. It might even mean the end
of my career—such as it was. Perhaps that would be no bad
thing. After all, if I were truly honest with myself, I knew I
was poorly suited to the work. I could go days without really
talking to anyone apart from my patients. My ability to dis-
tinguish between the normal, the eccentric, and the unwell
was itself highly compromised. And each succeeding event of
the past couple of days had further distorted my horizon, ever
more profoundly. Was it Abby's death that had done this? The
photo D'Angelo had given me was still in my pocket. I took it
out. Again she stared at me. A frozen image, detached from
the flow of action, always had an uncanny presence.

Eventually I made up a bed for myself in the front room
with some spare blankets, and turned the light off. I lay there
on the hard floorboards, unable to sleep, staring into the
dark. I was wondering about the Stevens Institute. Seeing the
guards at the door had jolted a memory. A couple of years
back, I'd bumped into an old classmate, somewhere in Murray Hill. We'd been psychiatry interns together at Bellevue.
He was in uniform, and I'd asked him what he was up to. He'd
said that he'd been working at a military hospital. Setting up
an experimental unit there. He'd been vague on the details,
and whatever he'd told me about it, I'd long forgotten. In any
case, that chance meeting came to mind now, when I thought
about the Stevens Institute. Had I heard that name from him?
Perhaps that was why it had seemed vaguely familiar to me.

I could hear the hesitant snore. I wasn't alone anymore;
there was this person in my bedroom. With luck, I'd find out
who he really was tomorrow. Or perhaps the mystery would
only deepen. He didn't seem real, in some indefinable way he
didn't even seem like the man I'd had committed. The various

threads of thought running through my mind refused to co-here: it was the problem of having no perspective, nothing to measure myself against. In the solitude, in the darkness, it was too easy to lose one's bearings.

The night wore on interminably. I'd left my wristwatch in the bathroom and the clock was in the bedroom; I couldn't tell if I'd been lying awake for an hour or for five. Tiredness weighed my body down until it felt like solid lead but con-sciousness wouldn't let go of me. At some point I entered an exhausted, disembodied state, neither wakefulness nor sleep. Thoughts became disconnected, dissolved into nightmarish abstraction. It felt as if the deeper I reached into myself, the less I found.

6

The light filtered through the grime of the windowpane and into my eyes. I sat bolt upright. Something was wrong: it was the silence—the absolute silence. I got up, went through to the bedroom. The man was laid out on the bed with his arms by his side, as if a mortician had positioned him like that. In shock, I grabbed his wrist. A weakish pulse—not dead, thank God. Body warm enough; the breathing soundless, irregular. I shook him gently, then more vigorously. He made a noise, a murmur, but didn't wake up. He wasn't just sleeping; he'd slipped into some sort of coma. The man was in my bedroom, on my bed, wearing my pajamas. I stood staring at him for a minute or two, at a loss as to what to do.

I went back to the front room, and hunted around for cigarettes. At the back of a kitchen drawer I found an ancient packet, along with a book of matches on which the name "Le Zinc" was printed. The French café where Abby and I used to meet up. I was lighting my cigarette with matches from a place that no longer existed. The harsh, stale taste of the cigarette and flow of nicotine jerked me temporarily out of the shock, back into the world. Of course, the fact that he'd gone into a coma wasn't at all unlikely, I reasoned. The man had had so many barbiturates over the past couple of days. Totally abnormal amounts, compared with what they did in the psychiatric wards I knew. At those levels, dosage was hardly an exact science. I should never have left him alone in the room; I should have monitored him throughout the night. I should have had a shot of adrenaline at the ready. I should have called an ambulance, I should have done any number of things. Instead, I'd lain on the floor next door, lost in a haze of nonsleep.

I could still do all those things. I could still go down to the pharmacy, write myself an adrenaline script. I could still call an ambulance. Perhaps I would. But for the moment, I felt incapable of movement, like in a dream. I wondered what would happen if I did nothing at all. The man had murmured when I'd shaken him, which meant it wasn't a profound coma. It would probably bottom out. He would resurface, regain consciousness sometime in the next few hours. Then again, it could also go the other way. He could fall further in, ever deeper, until finally he stopped breathing. I thought back to other coma patients I'd dealt with, as a young intern. There'd been a man, mid-fifties, who'd been unconscious for forty-eight hours following a stroke. He'd spent a month in the hospital, slowly recovering. Then came the day to leave. He'd carefully dressed himself and said goodbye to the nurses. As he'd walked haltingly out into the main hall, he'd turned, stopped, and said: "I think I'm going to die now." He'd dropped on the spot.

The silence of the room was broken by the faint sound of barrel-organ music, borne on the wind and distorted by it. Sitting at the table smoking, I could see the lower half of the man's body on the bed, or at least the shape of it under

the blankets, looming in the half-light. I remembered helping him out of the Stevens Institute. It felt choreographed
now, the way it had all happened, the way the cab had turned
up at the exact instant I'd needed it. I'd said to the man: "I'll
help you."

I smoked one cigarette after another until I finished the
packet. I stared at the matchbook and suddenly a fantasy I'd
once entertained after Abby had left came back—of her being
murdered, and me hunting down the murderer. The perfect
fantasy, allowing my ultimate revenge on her, and then saving
her as well.

I finally forced myself to go back and check on him. I did a
reflex test, got him to murmur again. I persuaded myself that
he'd come out of it well enough, without further intervention.
Could I trust my own judgment, though? Wasn't it a little
too convenient to think that nothing needed to be done? The
sound of the ringing phone tore through the morning, pulling me out of my self-absorption. I waited for it to stop, but it
rang on and on until I could bear it no more and I picked up
the receiver.

"Dr. Manne?"

"Yes."

"It's Mrs. Esterhazy here. Excuse me for calling you at
home. But I went to pick up my husband from the hospital
this morning. They told me you'd taken him away, last night."

"How did you get my number?"

"They gave it to me, at the hospital. They told me to call you."

"I see. Yes, he's under my care at the moment."

"Where is he, Doctor? When can I see him? When can he
come home?"

"Where are you? Are you still at the hospital?"

"No. I'm at home."

"Downtown? Where we met before?"

"That's right."

"Can I ask you a question? When did you last see your husband?"

"I visited him yesterday afternoon. At the hospital. That's when they told me he could leave today."

"You're sure it was him?"

"I . . . Of course I'm sure."

"Will you be at home for the next hour or so?"

"Yes."

"I'll be over right away. We have to talk."

I put down the receiver, but then immediately picked it up again, and dialed my office number.

"Miss Stearn. I'm afraid I'm still unwell. I won't be coming in today. Could you please cancel my appointments for the day?"

I could hear the surprise and uncertainty in her voice as she replied. It was true that in the two or three years she'd worked for me, I hadn't so much as taken an afternoon off, not until last Friday. But her astonishment somehow goaded me on, and without having quite thought it through, I heard myself continuing, "In fact, my doctor told me that what I need is complete rest. I think it would be for the best if you canceled my appointments for the next two weeks. As it is, I don't think I have much scheduled after the current week."

"Yes, but . . . of course, but . . . what will I do, Doctor? I mean, while you're not here?"

"This week, I'm sure there are administrative duties to keep you occupied. Next week . . . didn't you say something about a wedding in California? Your sister or something?"

"You told me you couldn't give me the time off."

"I've changed my mind. Take a week's paid leave."

I showered and dressed in minutes, in a daze. So that was it. I'd told my secretary I was off for two weeks, but the fact was that I'd finished with my office, my practice. A wave of conflicting emotions hit me. Relief, anxiety. Again that sense of the insubstantiality of things. I made one last check on the man in my bed. No real change, although his breathing seemed a little more regular now. I imagined him waking up in a strange room, in strange clothes, projected into another life, wondering what on earth had happened to him. I should leave him a note, perhaps. I cast around for pen and paper, but couldn't find anything. What could I write, in any case? In all probability I'd be back—with or without Mrs. Ester-hazy—before he awoke. But what if I were wrong? What if he woke up, and simply walked out of my apartment, swallowed up by the city? There would be something perfect about that. He couldn't do it, though, because once I'd left, and locked the door behind me, he'd be unable to get out. I fished around in a drawer for the spare key, which I placed on the small table by the entrance, where he couldn't miss it. I hardly wanted to be accused of holding a man in my apartment against his will, on top of everything else.

On the way out, I opened my mailbox in the lobby. It was part of my morning ritual, and I only realized its absurdity once I'd done it. I pulled out a black-bordered card with the details of Abby's funeral. Tomorrow morning, at a church on the Upper West Side. Speelman had scrawled something over the top: "I have an urgent matter to discuss with you. If you can't be at the funeral, please call me on the number below."

I was walking toward the subway. I was floating, in shock from the events of the past thirty-six hours. The sun had climbed over the buildings opposite, its harsh light expos-ing the city with an implacable clarity. Despite the noise and movement, the street seemed silent and static, as if certain re-ceptors inside me had been switched off. I had the impression that the passing people might be actors, precisely reenacting some day that had happened maybe sixty years before. An old man was walking down the street. Decades ago, he'd been a young man, perhaps walking down the same street. A mother was pushing a baby in a pram. Far from being newborn, the baby looked impossibly ancient. Street lamps, fire hydrants, traffic lights—all stage trappings, placed here and there, geometric objects without meaning.

Once I'd entered the subway, the shock dissipated again. Now I was filled with practical concerns. What was I going to say to Mrs. Esterhazy? Would she tell me anything about the man in my apartment? I wondered whether her phone call hadn't been some kind of ploy, to get me to leave the house. After all, how had she even gotten hold of my home number? The hospital certainly wouldn't have had it.

I fished about in my pocket for a nickel for the turnstile. My wallet was in there, but it felt bulkier than usual. I pulled it out, and was momentarily puzzled to see that it wasn't mine. It must belong to the man in my bed: I had the vaguest of memories of seeing it on his bedside table at the Stevens Institute, and sweeping it into my pocket while trying to help him up. I looked inside: a couple of dollar bills, various business cards, a phone number scribbled on a scrap of paper, receipts, a social security card in the name of Smith. There was a photo as well. A passport-sized picture of a smiling young woman. The kind you might well keep in your wallet, of your wife or fiancée. Judging by the hairstyle, it dated from before the war. But it wasn't Mrs. Esterhazy, I was sure of that. I closed the wallet and shoved it back deep in my pocket—I'd study the contents more carefully later. I wondered what I'd done with my own wallet, and then saw it in my mind's eye, sitting on the bathroom shelf, beside the water glass and toothbrush.

I was heading toward the platform, jostling through the thousands of people on the way to their offices. I, too, had an office. I had patients I'd been scheduled to see, whom my secretary was probably at this very moment phoning, to cancel the appointments. I couldn't think of them right now. They belonged to another life, a former existence. The mystery into which I'd been plunged, the Esterhazy case, that was what seemed real. I jerked my head around. All of a sudden I thought I'd caught a glimpse of the man in the fedora a few steps behind me. I'd have turned back and tried to catch him, if I hadn't been practically borne forward by the tide of people moving along the platform. The downtown train was twisting its way along a curve, heading into the station, almost insect-like with its two beaming headlights. I was standing right at the edge now. Hands lightly pressed against my back. With the train only yards from me, they gave a violent shove. I fought it for a second or two, tried to keep my balance, grabbed at the passengers beside me. The train headlights dazzled me. The moment seemed to stretch out into eternity. The image in my mind was that of the café where Abby and I used to go, the one that was now something else. Everything had once been something else.

Then I let go, and swung off into the emptiness.

PART TWO

I

My eyes opened to a blazing whiteness. After a minute or two of accustoming myself to the light, I saw that I was staring up at a ceiling. Later, I realized that I was only seeing out of one eye. I experimentally moved a hand to the left side of my face and touched some material. With difficulty I turned my head, one way, then the other. I was wearing a pale green open gown; there was a drip in my other arm. The room was empty, other than the bed I was in, a bedside table with nothing on it, and the drip stand. I supposed that the drip contained some sort of sedative, since when I came to, I'd felt deadened, cotton-headed, unable to think clearly. It wasn't necessarily an unpleasant feeling. At the same time, I was aware of something darker at my periphery. An anguish, which remained just out of reach.

The door opened. A nurse and a male orderly came in. I struggled to sit up, say something, but nothing would come out. The orderly stood by the door while the nurse expertly gave me a bed bath then eased me onto the bedpan. I had the impression she'd done this to me before, many times even, only I'd been too drugged to notice. When it was all done, I tried to speak again. The nurse smiled, shook her head and said: "There'll be plenty of time for that later." She inspected the bandage on my head, wrote something on a clipboard, then went out again. Once she'd gone, I lay there replaying the whole sequence of events in my mind. I kept repeating to myself her sole utterance: "There'll be plenty of time for that later."

Over the next few days, the periods of consciousness became longer, my powers of reasoning sharper. A dull ache in my left temple was with me almost permanently. I'd had a head injury, that much was obvious. I assumed that they'd been keeping me in an induced coma, and were now letting me come out of it gradually, with the sedation increasingly lighter each day. In my bed, in this blank room, I felt almost fetal.

A week or so passed. By now, I was usually awake when the nurse came to wash and administer to me. She'd also started bringing some sort of broth, which she said I was to eat, although I rarely felt hungry. I was thin, far thinner than I'd been before my hospitalization. Sometimes I'd catch sight of my spindly legs or arms and feel a surprise and almost a disgust that they were mine. My powers of speech were returning; I could answer the nurse's simple questions, formulate my own. But speaking had become something of an ordeal. Every time I started to say something, I couldn't shake the feeling that someone was there beside me, throwing his voice, making it appear to come out of my own mouth, but in a way that was not quite synchronized. I'd hesitate after the first word or two, disorientated by this effect, and it was some time before I could rid myself of the illusion.

A doctor came with the nurse one morning. With his

pince-nez and gray, pointed beard, he was the caricature of
the aging physician—just as the nurse, too, seemed to be a
caricature, with her brisk manner, matronly bust, hair se-
verely pinned back. She undid my bandages and the doctor
inspected my head, without addressing a word to me. He
murmured something to the nurse, and then abruptly disappeared. The nurse carried on washing me as usual. At first I'd
thought the doctor had simply gone to the corridor to grab
something, as the examination had been so extremely brief.
But once the nurse had finished washing me, she too left, and
I was alone once more.

How long had I been here? I guessed at least a couple of
weeks, but it might just as well have been a couple of months.
Whenever I'd asked the nurse anything beyond the immediately practical, she'd quickly shut me up with one or another
of her trite phrases: "There'll be plenty of time for that later"
or "You must rest up and not tire yourself out with all these
questions." After a few days of this I'd decided to be persistent
about one thing at least. I wanted to see my face. And now
every time the nurse came, I asked for a mirror. At first she
smiled and shook her head. Later, she became annoyed, and
in the end she simply ignored the request. But then, just when
I'd given up hope, she appeared one morning and produced
a compact mirror.

A queasy dread invaded me as the nurse unwound the
bandage from the left side of my face. And yet with that
first glance in the small mirror, the initial reaction was relief. It didn't seem as bad as I'd feared. My left temple had
been shaved and there was a line of staples across the side of
my head. It looked gruesome, but once the staples were removed and my hair had grown back, there probably wouldn't
be anything to see. Worse, though, was the scar that split
my cheek. It hadn't healed well—the damaged skin hadn't

properly knitted together. Why had they stapled my head, but not stitched up my cheek? The scar was surrounded by big red blotches. Perhaps the wound had become too infected to stitch. In time, the blotches would fade, the scar too. In a few months, my face probably wouldn't look too awful. It wouldn't be the same, either. It didn't have the same balance as before. When I tried out various expressions, they came out different. Staring into the mirror, all I could feel was puzzlement. Not because my face now looked like somebody else's, but because I felt strangely myself.

Memories came back slowly, in haphazard fashion, as one might blindly pull balls from a bag. The feelings returned first. One morning I awoke overwhelmed with sadness. Only hours later did Abby's death come back to me. Long after I'd been struck by a horrified bewilderment, the image of the comatose man in my apartment flashed into my mind. When I finally recalled the push onto the subway tracks, my terror was mixed with a sense of liberation that I was at a loss to explain to myself.

My world had shrunk to this bare room. Strange to think that outside the door, the life of the hospital went on. And that beyond that, there was a city with its millions of people, whose fates were utterly unconnected to mine. A small window that looked onto a courtyard was my sole evidence of this outside world. Sometimes, even it felt as if it were not an opening but a screen onto which images were being projected. Sitting up I could see French windows opposite, leading onto a tiny balcony with an equally tiny washing line. Every morning, a woman in a housecoat would fling the windows open. She had a trim figure and dark hair in a bob; I imagined her to be in her early thirties, but actually she was too far away for me to tell. There'd be days on which she'd hang out washing. Other days, she'd simply stand on the balcony only large enough for one person, and stare out, smoking a cigarette. I fancied I could perceive a certain reflective melancholy in her as she smoked, staring out onto the courtyard below. From those ten minutes she spent on the balcony each morning, I tried to construct a life. Judging from the clothes on the washing line, I supposed that she had a husband and a small boy, although I never saw them either. I imagined her in the morning, busily preparing her husband's breakfast, and getting her son ready for school. And then when she'd finally sent them both out the door, that's when she'd come on the balcony. It would be her time. A moment of respite before the day properly got going, before washing the breakfast things, the housework, perhaps some menial job to go to. Her few minutes of withdrawal, of blanking out the drudgery of life.

The drip was removed. The periods during which I could sit up without inducing nausea or dizziness became longer. One day I decided to try getting up from my bed. On my feet, I felt fragile, lightheaded, but nothing more. I took a few experimental steps, and found myself by the door. Without thinking I tried the handle—locked. I returned to my bed, exhausted by my little expedition.

The doctor came again, unannounced. This time he stayed longer. He looked at my head, listened to my heart with his stethoscope, asked me to breathe in and out, tapped me here and there to test my reactions. It felt perfunctory, as if he were simply putting on a performance for me. Once he'd finished, he stood there in silence for a minute or so, leaving me perplexed. Finally, he said: "When you sit up, do you feel dizzy?"

"Less and less so."

"Could you sit up now? Good. I'm going to ask you a few questions. First, what is your name?"

"Surely you have all my details already."

"Just answer the question, please. Your name."

"David Frederick Manne."

"Where do you live?"

"353 East Fifty-Sixth Street."

"How old are you?"

"Thirty-three."

"What is your profession?"

"I'm a doctor of medicine, in private practice."

"What year is it?"

"1949."

"What month?"

"September I think. No, probably October. To be honest, I'm not sure how long I've been here."

"All right. Thank you."

Again he stood there in silence for a good moment, as if wondering what to do next. He rummaged about in his pocket. Eventually he drew out a small photograph and showed it to me. "Do you know who this is?"

A young woman, late twenties perhaps. Nothing remarkable about her face, and I certainly didn't recognize her. Nonetheless there was something odd about the photograph. It was her hairstyle, old-fashioned for a girl her age. It occurred to me that the photograph itself must be fairly old. I shook my head.

"I don't know who it is."

"You're sure?"

"I'm sure."

The doctor started to leave. "Keep the photograph. Perhaps you'll remember something about it later on."

"Wait a minute. You haven't told me anything. What's the photograph got to do with me? I want to know how long I'm going to be in here. I want to know how serious my injuries are. I'm a doctor too, you know. You can tell me."

He had his hand on the door handle; he turned briefly

toward me. "Don't worry. There will be plenty of time for that later."

Before I had time to protest any further, he was gone. I felt a quick of stab of anger at the peremptory way he'd treated me. What an absurd figure, with his pointed beard, his pocket watch, his superannuated accent, his ponderous manner! But the anger quickly died, leaving behind a residue of disquiet. I struggled to my feet, hobbled to the door. Locked again.

Back on my bed, I closed my eyes and waited for my heartbeat to slow to its normal rhythm. This whole charade with the doctor flagged up a possibility that hadn't occurred to me. Perhaps the hospital *hadn't* known who I was. Perhaps the doctor really had been fishing for answers. If so, I'd set him straight, at least. Now they knew my identity, wheels would surely be set in motion. I opened my eyes again, almost surprised to see the ceiling, the walls, the bedside table. There was something notional about this attenuated existence in a hospital room—a reality my brain didn't necessarily want to believe in. When the nurse came back, I'd have it out with her. I'd ask about the locked door. I'd ask to see another doctor. I'd need to speak to the police as well, of course. It was quite outrageous. I hadn't even been told which hospital I was in.

No one came. They seemed so random, the nurse's visits, I could never tell when they would be, and they always felt like an unexpected interruption. Outside, the light was fading. It would be night soon, and I would sleep, a dreamless sleep as always. Then in the morning, I'd see the woman on the balcony. Unlike the nurse and doctor, she was entirely predictable, always there at the right moment. How did I know that? I had no clock in the room. It might just as well be the nurse's appearances that were regular, and those of the woman on the balcony were random.

When I did wake up, sometime in what I presumed to be

morning, I found myself with a drip in my arm again. I pulled it out and pressed my hand to where the needle had been, to staunch any bleeding, but there didn't seem to be any. I managed to sit myself up and stared through the tiny window for what felt like hours, but the woman didn't appear on the balcony. I knew she wouldn't; I'd missed her. I'd slept right through her.

2

The doctor visited several times over the following days. There were more medical examinations, which became increasingly cursory. Afterward, he'd take out a notebook and ask me questions. Where I was born, where I was educated, where my office was. At some seemingly arbitrary moment, he'd put the notebook away and leave. At first, I'd answered quite passively. The whole setup—the doctor-caricature, the emptiness of the room and its unremitting whiteness—pushed me toward apathy, acquiescence. But on the fourth or fifth visit, I lost my temper. "Enough of the questions," I said, "I want answers. I want to know where I am, why my door is always locked. I want to know what my prognosis is. I need to see the police." Suddenly I found myself in a rage, almost screaming. Out of nowhere, a couple of male orderlies appeared. I hadn't laid a finger on the doctor, had done nothing beyond raising my voice, but they pinned me down on my bed. I felt a prick on my arm, then nothing.

The visits continued. We carried on as if the incident

hadn't happened. In truth, I was embarrassed by it, which in
turn made me more compliant. I remembered the infantile
outbursts of patients—born of confinement and impotence—
from my time as an intern. Almost every long-term patient
had them at one point or another. And then afterward, they'd
be embarrassed, docile, just as I had been. I remembered, too,
the patients' constant quest for more information, and the
doctors' constant reluctance to part with any, lest it be mis-
construed, used against them. I'd spent so many hundreds of
hours in hospitals, but never before as a patient. It was unsettling to be on the other side of the equation.

The interrogations, too, continued. Perplexed, at a loss
as to how to respond, I figured I'd simply bide my time, until the shape of my circumstances became clearer. By now,
we'd exhausted the simple facts of my life. We'd moved on to
the minutiae. What subjects I'd enjoyed at school, who my
friends were, where I went on vacation, what I did with my
spare time. My professional life; my sexual life. The experience of being relentlessly questioned was mesmerizing. It was
boring, and yet unsettling. The doctor was coming every day
now, sometimes in the morning, sometimes in the afternoon.
Each time he stayed longer. We were down to novels I liked,
cars I'd driven, the layout of my apartment. Occasionally the
doctor would press me for more detail on a particular subject,
for no apparent reason: I'd start to approximate, to fabricate.
Then after he'd gone, the bits and pieces of our conversation
would filter back through my mind, blend together, distort,
like fragments of a dream that lingered well into the waking
hours.

Could this banal accumulation of facts really be a life, my
life? If so, it seemed a poor thing, lacking all imagination. The
interrogations had left me feeling alienated from my past, as
though it were in fact someone else's. One of my patients',

perhaps. Indeed, it had occurred to me that my interrogator was much more of a psychiatrist than a hospital doctor. And why ever not? I looked at myself in the compact mirror that the nurse had left me. I'd changed, certainly. From a reasonably attractive man to an odd-looking one. From an active professional, to an invalid, confined to bed. Each change had closed doors to myriad futures that would now never be. I picked up the photograph the doctor had left me, of the young woman. I'd worked it out now, of course. It had been in the wallet that I'd taken from the man in my apartment, and stuffed in my pocket. They'd found it on me.

Biographical detail was the glinting, hard surface, reflecting meaning away from the subject. It said nothing of a life, the inner life, the real life. I remembered sifting through the jumble of papers my parents had left behind after they'd died—my aunt and uncle had ceremoniously handed me the box on my eighteenth birthday. Birth certificates; old passports; train tickets; receipts for important purchases; worthless bonds; ancient photos of people I couldn't identify; letters from relatives I didn't know, replete with references to events of great significance at the time, now sunk into obscurity. I'd been too young to remember my parents when they were alive, and they'd rarely been alluded to as I was growing up. An outline of their lives might be surmised from this detritus, but I would never have a feeling for who they'd been.

I looked out into the courtyard and the building opposite. I could often sense when the woman on the balcony was about to appear, and sure enough, a few moments later, there she was. Shaking her head of black hair, reaching for the packet of cigarettes from the pocket of her housecoat. Staring out once again into the void. Other people's lives were impossibly mysterious, when one knew nothing of them. She looked European to me, but since I could make out so little

of her, this could only be whimsy. Nevertheless, on this slender thread I'd begun to construct a story, one that became
increasingly embellished each time I saw her. She was a war
refugee. Perhaps her husband had been killed in action. Or
executed for treason. Or for resistance activities. She'd somehow managed to escape, to make it to New York, where she
knew nobody. An immigrant with little English, and a child
to care for, she'd had few options but to find herself a new
husband, which eventually she did. A kindly, older man, prepared not only to marry her but provide for a child that was
not his own. The woman had grown fond of her husband, but
she could never bring herself to love him. The ghost of her
former husband was there, although in what form I didn't yet
know . . . I would lose myself in this invention for minutes at
a time. Of course, I could always pull back when I wanted to.
I knew well enough that the intensity of this vision—its sheer
realness—was illusory. I knew that when I finally left the hospital, if I went knocking on her door, I'd find someone quite
different, just an ordinary-looking Manhattan housewife, no
tragic past, not elegantly blowing smoke into the emptiness of
the city.

"Now, tell me about your wife."

The words shook me. My marriage had barely been mentioned in conversations with the doctor until now, even
though I'd talked in some detail about my occasional affairs
since the divorce. I couldn't even remember if I'd told him
that Abby was dead. An image of her floated into my mind,
somewhere in the mental distance.

"What's there to say? I was married once. But only briefly.
A long time ago."

"What was she like? Describe her to me."

"Tall. Brunette. She was an actress. Always looked very self-assured. Confident on stage.

"But elsewhere?"

"In other ways she could be less assured."

"How?"

"She was the one who'd wanted to get married. We were much too young. Anyone could have seen we weren't right for each other. But I was infatuated. And she'd needed that anchor, for a time."

"Do you attach any importance to the fact that she was an actress?"

"How do you mean?"

The doctor didn't elaborate. Sometimes he'd leave these silences, and I'd feel forced to fill them.

"She was an actress, it was what she did. In the same way that practicing medicine is what you do. That's all."

What was he driving at? It felt like we were engaged in a game. The subject at hand—whether it be Abby or anything else—was of no importance. Only rules and tactics mattered. When the routine of his questioning set in, when I felt that I knew exactly what he was going to ask, that was the moment he'd stump me. I tried to imagine what kind of inner life the doctor might have, but I couldn't easily. No doubt he had a wife, children, and all the usual cares and worries. But to me, he existed merely as a foil.

He straightened his things, made as if to leave. Before doing so, he took a notepad from his briefcase and handed it to me, along with a pencil. "Here, have this. I want you to write down whatever comes to your mind about your wife—your former wife. All right?"

"All right."

Once he'd gone, I could feel myself passing through the now-familiar sequence of emotional states: anger, disquiet, anxiety, puzzlement, contemplation. And then finally, a profound introspection. The outside world had its borders and demarcations, but this interior one was boundless. One could always go further and further inside, the retreat could never be complete. I stared at the pencil in my hand for minutes on end, as if it were an alien object. I remembered hospitals where I'd worked, and how when patients asked for something to write with, they were always given pencils and not pens. Why? Because pens were more messy? Because they might conceivably be used as weapons? Some department had probably issued a directive about it last century, I mused, setting in stone a practice that would remain for decades to come, simply because there was no particular reason to change it. How much of life was like that?

I wondered why the doctor had suddenly brought up the subject of Abby. From my experience as a psychiatrist, what mattered most in any patient's narrative were the things left out. When these things were eventually mentioned—by the doctor or the patient—it was an attempt to inoculate the story against them. I looked down at the blank pages of the notepad. There was no reason why I should obey the doctor and write anything about Abby, but I felt somehow compelled to do so.

I see you now. You're clearer than ever to me, even as I become obscure to myself. Our decade-long estrangement has made you more vivid, not less.

You once told me that at the age of sixteen, you'd felt halfway through life, regardless of when you might die. It turns out you were literally correct. Your premonition haunts me. Your early death casts a black light over the landscape. Every memory of you has to be reconsidered, revised, under that light. An old man on his deathbed is the finished work of his past, but you, in dying young, remain a hypothesis. You are the years never lived.

You died childless. You told me that you wanted children, when you were older, when you'd made your mark in the theater. Instead, a tumor grew in you, and expanded until it took your life. Sixty years from now, who will think of you, who will talk about you? We are truly dead when there is no one left to remember us, when our children and grandchildren are gone as well. We who are childless die sooner than the others.

You had a best friend when you were ten or eleven. Her name was Susan. You'd become friends at school when you'd discovered that you were born on the same day. For a few months, you'd done everything together. You used to pretend you were twins. Then summer came, and your friend's family went upstate on vacation. They rented a house on a lake. You were going to join them in the second week. But before you could get there, your friend had gone out on the lake in a canoe, without telling anyone. The canoe had overturned and your friend had drowned. You only told me this story once. It was when you were about to visit her parents. They'd never gotten over the death of their daughter. You visited them out of pity, but only infrequently. They saw you as a continuation of their daughter, which made you uncomfortable. Once, her father had even accidently called you Susan, which had spooked you. You'd felt like a ghost, you'd said.

It had all come out in an easy flow, when normally writing was a stuttering, painful business. I stopped suddenly. It struck me that I was writing in the second person, and I

wondered why. The thought interrupted my flow, and I knew
I'd never get it back again. I looked up from the notepad. The
woman was on the balcony. She was smoking, as usual, but
instead of staring out into the city, she was looking in my
direction. She'd been watching me writing. I felt transfixed as
my eyes locked into her gaze. Eventually she brought a hand
up to her forehead, as if to brush something away, or pat down
her hair. She turned, momentarily contemplated a streetscape
I couldn't see from my angle, then went back inside. It had all
taken place in the space of thirty seconds at most.

I waited for my muscles to relax again. I continued to
stare through the window. She'd left the door onto the balcony slightly ajar, even though it must be chilly outside now,
with fall well underway; it felt like a strange sort of invitation.
The moment was barely over, but I was already reliving it in
my mind. My looking up to see her eyes, boring into mine.
I wondered whether perhaps I served the same function in
her life that she served in mine. Was it me she came out on
the balcony to see? Was she making up stories about me? She
sees a youngish man lying on a hospital bed, half of his face
bandaged, always staring out the window. He's there, day and
night, always gazing out. It would be natural to wonder what
had brought him there, wouldn't it? It would be a mystery,
perfect material for fantasy.

The next day, the doctor was back as usual. I handed him the
pages I'd written about Abby. He looked over them briefly,
not long enough to read them properly, then gave them back
to me. Whatever the purpose of getting me to write something, it patently wasn't so that he could read it. He leaned
over, gently unwrapped the bandage on my head, examined
the wound.

"The staples will have to come out. I'll get someone to see you about that."

"Okay."

"Do you remember how you got it, this wound? Do you remember anything?"

I'd seen it coming, this discussion about my injury and the "accident," as I termed it in my mind, even though it had been no accident at all. I knew that broaching the subject of Abby had been a harbinger, clearing the way.

"Yes, I do remember. I was on the subway platform. The station was . . ."

"Lexington and Fifty-Ninth."

"That's right. It was morning, peak hour. Very crowded. As I was going down the stairs, I noticed someone. I'd seen him before. He'd been following me, at least I thought so. Then I was down on the platform. The train was coming. I could see it down the tunnel. I felt someone prod me from behind. Tentative at first. I turned around. I thought it might be a friend or something. Or did I? I can't remember. No, I don't think I turned around. There was this prod, then an almighty shove. I lost my balance, fell onto the track. That's all I remember."

"You blacked out."

"I don't know. I don't remember any more. I guess the train hit me."

"This fellow, the one who'd been following you, the one you think pushed you. Do you know who he was?"

"I'd seen him before. I don't know who he is."

"Do you know why he might have pushed you?"

I was silent for a moment. "Forgive me, but I think the time's come for me to speak to the police. About this, and other matters. I've asked you before, but you haven't . . . perhaps you thought I needed time to recover. I've recovered sufficiently now. There are important matters I need to discuss with the police."

The doctor had his hand to his chin, in a reflective pose. He didn't seem to have heard what I'd said, or in any case, didn't respond to it.

"This man. Are you certain he pushed you?"

"I was pushed. Whether it was by the man I noticed beforehand, I can't say for sure."

"I see. There were a lot of witnesses, you know. A lot of statements were taken."

"I imagine so."

"They were all of the impression that you jumped. Of your own accord. No one mentioned seeing you being pushed."

"What can I say? It was crowded. It mightn't have been obvious to other people. But I was pushed."

"Witnesses said they saw you come flying down the stairs, directly throwing yourself in front of the train."

"No. It wasn't like that. I was standing on the platform by the rails. I was pushed."

"I see." The doctor sat wordlessly for a minute or two, observing me. He gestured to the photograph that still sat on my bedside table. "Anything come back to you about the photograph? Any memories of who she might be?"

"I have some notions about the photograph, yes. I'm not prepared to say anything right now. I've told you, I want to see the police. I've said to you several times, on several different occasions. I've had enough of this charade now. It's time you called the police." I looked expectantly at the doctor, but he said nothing, simply continued watching me. "I'm being kept here against my will. The door to my room is locked. I demand to know why. If you're my doctor, then you're guilty of gross misconduct. There'll be consequences, I'll make sure of it."

I was getting worked up; I'd raised my voice. At the same time, I tried to control my anger; I didn't want a repeat of that business with the orderlies.

"Do you know why you're here? Take a look at these."

He took some papers from his case and pushed them across to me. I quickly glanced through them.

"Committal papers. For a man named Stephen Smith."

"Does the name mean anything to you?"

"Possibly."

"Might he have any connection with you?"

"It's a very common-sounding name. He may have been a patient of mine. If so, I see it wasn't me who committed him. I'm getting tired of the games. Could you please tell me what the relevance of all this is?"

"Well. I'll outline what I know about Stephen Smith, if you like. He's a drifter. Born in Dayton, Ohio. Found his way to New York at some unspecified time, probably about a decade ago. Since then he's been in and out of menial work. Sometimes lodging in boarding houses, sometimes sleeping on the streets. He's been picked up for vagrancy at least twice. He spent six weeks in a mental institution three years ago. Now he's back in one, after a suicide attempt."

"What's the point of this farce? What are you trying to prove?"

"Now . . . try to stay calm. Please take your hands off me."

I'd leaned forward and gripped the doctor's arm. I'd done it without even noticing. I backed off, in a daze.

"I'm going to leave you a couple of pages from the file. Have a good look at them. Someone will be in to see you in an hour or so. All right?"

I didn't say anything. The doctor moved to the door, slowly, deliberately, as though he were in a stable with a horse he didn't want to frighten. As he opened it, I glimpsed a couple of orderlies waiting on either side. The door clicked shut, and I could hear the turn of the key. I sprang out of bed. It was as if I were watching myself at the door, about to hammer at it. But then I had an attack of dizziness. Stars were in my eyes and my body went limp. It was all I could do to haul myself back onto the bed and lie down, stare up.

White ceiling, white walls. Nothing changed. Beside me were the papers the doctor had left me. After a period of just lying there, I picked them up, and listlessly scanned them. "Serious, nonfatal head injuries . . . identified from social security card on his person . . . second suicide attempt . . ." I put them down and closed my eyes, exhausted, and thinking of nothing.

3

From then on, the doctor-caricature with the pince-nez disappeared from my life. I was strapped to a gurney and wheeled to the operating room to get the staples out. When I came to from the anesthetic, a different doctor was leaning over me. Later, I found out his name: Dr. Peters. A man of around my own age and build, he came every morning and afternoon. For a few days I'd refused to talk to him, at first out of shock, then from anger and confusion. Once I'd regained some equilibrium, though, I changed tactics. By now it was clear enough that I was in a psychiatric hospital and I was more than familiar with the setup. There would be the padded cells for violent patients. The next step up would be my current situation: confined to one's room. But patients who were docile and cooperative enough could spend their time in a communal hall, where there might be books, magazines, newspapers, perhaps a radio set or gramophone player.

"So. Where did you say you were you born?"

"Hackensack, New Jersey. A couple of years later I was sent to live with my aunt and uncle, on Long Island."

"Why was that?"

"My parents died."

"How did they die?"

"A theater fire. Here in Manhattan, if that's where I am. Quite a few people died in the fire. It was reported in the *Times*, if you'd care to check. I'm fairly sure the date was April 17, 1919."

Dr. Peters scribbled on his pad, although whether he was noting the date or something entirely different, I didn't know. He was making me go through the whole story of my life again. I'd wearily protested that I'd already done that, at some length, with the previous doctor, but he'd been adamant. And, like before, there'd always be some detail that interested him—my parents' death, for example—and we'd go over it again and again. I recognized the technique from police interrogations I'd seen with D'Angelo. I'd also occasionally used it myself. I'd make a patient obsessively go over some aspect of his narrative—it almost didn't matter which—until eventually, in the retelling, and the retelling of the retelling, its fault line would reveal itself.

The same story, told in the same words. But after a while it isn't the same. With repetition, a story loses its flavor, stops feeling like the truth, stops *being* true. It's just another performance. Why had I been so keen to give the date of the report on the theater fire in the *Times*? I'd once discussed the subject of police interrogations with D'Angelo: if there are *no* holes in a story, he'd said, then generally it's not true. People who are telling the truth tend to be slipshod about it; they contradict themselves, forget crucial details. They have no ready answers when pulled up on their inconsistencies. The seamless narratives, where every loose thread is carefully woven back into the fabric—those are the suspect ones.

The doctor left. Later, there would be lunch, followed by a trip to the bathroom accompanied by an orderly—a brief yet intoxicating glimpse of the world beyond my room. But right now there was the bed, the white walls, the window, and myself. In the solitude of it all, my mind spun back. Faces of old patients from years ago returned to me, so clearly, and I wondered what had happened to them, how they'd fared in life, following my intervention. Why had I so rarely had the curiosity to find out? I recalled one of the few instances when I had indeed tried to follow up. A man in his fifties, excessively polite, who'd spent years working on intricate ink drawings of an imaginary city. They had a peculiar, ghostly quality, and he'd claimed that the images came to him in visions. I'd asked him where he thought the city was, and he'd said he didn't know, but that he imagined it was somewhere cold, and in Europe. He'd believed that he had a telepathic link with a person in this cold, European city. His theory had been that as he was having his visions, this other person would in turn be having visions of New York, seeing the city through his eyes. They would be mirroring each other.

Then one day a colleague who was originally from Sweden had come to see me. I had one of the drawings on my desk. "It's Stockholm," he'd said, and he'd pointed out landmarks he recognized. "And yet this building here, I remember it only as a boy. It was pulled down at least twenty years ago." For a few weeks, I'd become obsessed with this patient. I'd ascertained that he had no family connections with Sweden. That he had never been to Stockholm, had in fact never been out of the United States. I'd gone to the New York Public Library, taken out illustrated books on Stockholm, identified for myself various buildings in the drawings, mapped them out to persuade myself that there was a common viewpoint from which they'd all been executed. I'd entertained all sorts of increasingly far-fetched ideas about my patient and where the drawings had come from, ideas that went beyond mere psychiatry. I'd gotten myself in too deep: I was beginning to buy into my patient's story.

Eventually I'd managed to pull out of it, pull back. It had occurred to me that if I had been able to go to the library and look up images of Stockholm, then so had my patient, and that I needed no other explanation than that. The rest really was psychiatry. It was simply a question of whether my patient was a charlatan, or whether he actually was deluded, and if so, what to do about it. All this had struck me in a second, with the force of revelation.

I'd changed tack with my patient. Up until then, I'd been going along with him. I'd allowed him to tell his story without contradicting him, without passing judgment, without letting him know what I thought of it. Now I'd felt the time had come to take a more aggressive stance. As my secretary had shown him into my office, I'd scattered my desk with the pictures he'd drawn, together with some illustrated books on Stockholm, open on panoramic city views. I'd wordlessly pointed to various illustrations that were evidently models for his drawings.

"Amazing, amazing," he'd muttered under his breath.

"What's amazing? You've simply copied out these photographs, haven't you? Admit it!"

He would admit nothing. All he'd do was continue to shake his head and mutter, "Amazing!" A frustration rose in me; I'd abruptly stood up and berated him: "You know you copied these photographs! Admit it to me now! If you don't admit it, there'll be trouble!" My patient had looked up at me in fear and surprise, then clammed right up. I knew I wouldn't get anything more out of him that session, so I'd eventually called a halt twenty minutes early. All week, my failure had gnawed at me. It had been a silly idea to confront him like that. Of course, it was always a temptation to challenge one's patients. But it was rarely productive. Best to hold back, to approach things from oblique angles, to guide the patient slowly toward his error, as if he were discovering it by himself.

In preparation for his next appointment, I'd concocted an apology. I'd been too impatient; now I wanted start afresh with him, as it were, step back and take things at a slower pace. He'd always been a punctual man, and when he still hadn't turned up fifteen minutes into his session, I'd understood. He'd broken off the treatment. That happened often enough—patients suddenly disappearing, never to be seen again. It always left me feeling hollow, somehow forsaken, as if it had been me and not them who had been seeking therapy. These abandonments would normally take me days to recover from. I took this one even harder: for weeks, this patient had remained at the forefront of my mind, until one day I couldn't take it any more and I'd decided to take a trip out to where he lived, according to his file. I'd found myself outside a rooming house in a desolate corner of Red Hook. He wasn't there. The landlady had told me that he'd left a few weeks back, in other words at around the same time as he'd walked out on me. He'd simply taken off without a word, after years of living there, keeping pretty much to himself the whole time. He'd been scrupulously honest, though, pushing an envelope under the landlady's door with the rent he owed in it. "Did he leave anything behind?" I'd asked. The landlady had shaken her head. The room had been spotless; it was as if he'd never been there at all.

I'd sat there on my bed for some time, thinking about this former patient, a sadness once again invading me, eating into me. That last act, of leaving the money for the landlady even though he would never see her again, seemed so poignant, it nearly had me in tears. Curious how these faces from the past loomed up, crowding my mental theater, and were clearer to me than the actual people I saw every day—the doctor, the nurse, the orderlies. Why had I suddenly thought of the Stockholm man again, after all these years? I'd been wrong about him, and the core of his mystery remained.

My life since the subway accident had the dull passivity of a dream, with its unconnected events simply washing over me, one after the other. The long interrogation to which I'd been subjected over the days and weeks was an elaborate fiction. The doctor purported to believe what I was telling him, and I purported to accept that he was believing it. We'd become entrenched in our respective roles and the longer it went on, the harder it would be to break out of them. I recalled yet another case history. It was when I'd been at City Psychiatric. A long-term patient on my ward had died. He'd had no visitors for years, but we checked his file for next of kin, and found he had a sister. She'd been astonished to receive my call. Once she'd recovered from the shock, she'd told me that her brother had indeed been briefly detained at a New York mental hospital, but he'd been discharged years ago, and was now living somewhere out on the West Coast. What had happened, it transpired, was that at some point, probably during admission, our recently deceased patient's papers had been mixed up with this other person's. Why the patient had never protested, why he'd simply gone along with the sudden name change, would forever remain an enigma, since the error had gone undetected until his death.

From the reverse perspective, I could now see how easily such things could happen. There was something narcotic, almost hypnotizing about being a patient on a mental ward, whatever your state of mind. In this infantilizing context, you quickly became who and what people told you you were. The longer you were there, the less strength you had to stand up for any competing reality. It certainly shook me up, thinking about this old case. It sent a frisson of dread through me. Until now, I'd been content to leave things as they were with the doctor, to simply ride it out until I knew how I was to go on, confident that the truth would, in any case, eventually manifest itself. Now, I wasn't so sure.

The day had passed in the usual haze of memory and introspection, over before I'd been properly aware that it had even begun. It was twilight now. I always liked this half hour or so when the day was fading but they hadn't put the lights on in my room yet. It had been a favorite moment of mine in my Park Avenue office as well. I'd swivel around in my chair, staring through the blinds to the street below, with the eerie play of dying rays over the buildings. It spoke to something fundamentally ambiguous within me. Across the courtyard now, the light snapped on in the woman's apartment. Her curtains were drawn, but I could glimpse her body moving behind them, like some kind of shadow game. She appeared to be naked or in her underwear, as I could make out the scissor movement of her legs, the exaggerated curve of her breasts. Her figure seemed magnified, silhouetted against the fabric, by some trick of the light, each ripple of the curtain veiled with erotic possibility. Where was her child, her husband? Why did I never see them? I thought of the way she'd fixed me with her stare that one time, and wondered when it would happen again.

The doctor was back. I must have slept; it must be a new morning: the days ticked over, without my noticing. He was questioning me yet again about my parents—a strange subject to be stuck on, it seemed to me, since everything I knew about them was secondhand. I answered in automatic mode, my mind elsewhere. I noticed how the doctor would always move the chair in the room so it was just so, always at exactly the same angle to the bed, and then at the end of the interrogation, he'd move it back to how it had been, despite the fact that no one other than himself used it.

He had a neutral, professorial air to him and a disconnected manner, without it being overtly hostile. In some ways he was a version of myself, of what I might have been. When I'd been working at City Psychiatric, I'd been offered a full-time post, and I probably would have accepted it, but for Abby's influence. She'd pushed me into renting the Park Avenue office and getting myself started in private practice, despite my youth and lack of experience. She'd idealized my possibilities and talked me out of the safe route. If it hadn't been for her, I probably would have ended up pretty much like this Dr. Peters. A job in a teaching hospital, which would have eventually led to a more senior position, then perhaps research or lecturing work with a university, ultimately a professorship . . . How very different things might have been, I mused, had I never met Abby.

"What's the point of continuing with this, Doctor? Why go over and over the same ground?"

"I'm trying to help you. And if you can help me, by answering my questions, then the sooner we'll be able to . . ."

I cut him off. "I think we should be straight with each other. I don't understand why you replaced the other doctor without a word. Did he tell me something he shouldn't have? What does the name Stephen Smith mean to you?"

"Well . . . what does it mean to *you*?"

"I'll play that game, if you want. When you brought me in, you found a wallet in my pocket. In the wallet was the photo of the young woman you see over there. Also, I'm guessing, a social security card, in the name of Stephen Smith. Actually, I don't have a social security card. They don't issue them to doctors, as you know. The wallet was someone else's. A patient of mine, in fact. I imagine he can be easily traced. What I don't understand is why you simply accepted that I was this person. Why didn't you check further? It's unprofessional."

The doctor blinked. I could see him toying with his answer, wondering whether it was too late to guide our relationship back to safer waters, or whether the spell had been broken for good.

"You were identified by other means. I assure you."

"How could I have been? Have you looked into what I've been telling you? Have you spoken to anyone who knows me?"

"I've spoken to the doctor who treated you the last time you were brought in. He came to see you, while you were recovering. I've also talked to Dr. Manne's secretary."

I was quiet. I let that sink in. My body trembled: it had been since I'd first challenged the doctor. I couldn't imagine him and my secretary together in the same room, let alone talking to each other. It was as if they were from such different worlds that the encounter would be physically impossible.

"By the way," he continued, "can you tell me her name?"

"It's . . . she's . . . dammit!" I shook my head with frustration: in the tension of the moment, I just couldn't think. The way the doctor had mentioned "Dr. Manne" in the third person had stopped me cold. He was writing something—eyes down. Rarely did he make eye contact, in fact. He didn't ask me for my secretary's name again, and an ominous silence descended. Finally, I felt compelled to break it: "Why . . . what did she say?"

The doctor looked up now. Again, I could see the indecision

playing over his face, or I thought I could: perhaps that, too, was a performance.

"She doesn't remember your name. I've been unable to ascertain your connection with Dr. Manne. But my assumption is that you were once a patient of his. Unfortunately I don't have access to his papers. All the material in his office was impounded."

"Ask her to come here. She'll be able to identify me, at least. She'll be able to confirm that I am who I say I am."

Even as I said that, I felt an inward shiver. What if she came in, and for whatever bizarre reason, failed to identify me? But why would she? Then again, it was impossible to tell what might now happen. The kaleidoscope had been twisted. I was gazing out into a world that had the same form, but was wholly different.

"I very much doubt that she'd come. I had the greatest difficulty getting her talk with me as it is. She was quite distraught by the whole business of Dr. Manne's death."

"His what?"

Another silence, this time for a good long while. Even in my state of profound shock at what he'd just said, I could sense the doctor's great unease, his not knowing whether to stay put, or bring the meeting to an end. I knew from my time as a psychiatrist the feeling of a session spun out of control, of subjects long avoided suddenly erupting, like a banal conversation between lovers that randomly escalates into a vicious row.

"You say Dr. Manne is dead?"

"That's right."

"How can that be? Where's the body?"

"I only know what Dr. Manne's secretary was kind enough to tell me. The doctor hadn't returned to work from a two-week leave, and didn't answer his phone either. A few days later, his secretary called the police. For some reason, nothing was done for some time. Eventually the police gained entry into Manne's apartment and found him dead in his bed. There was an autopsy. He'd taken an overdose of barbiturates. Apparently he'd been depressed over the death of his ex-wife."

"Who was the police officer who found him? What was his name? Who identified the body?"

"I'm afraid I can't tell you. I mean, I don't know."

It was too dislocating to be talking of a "Dr. Manne" in the third person. I simply couldn't digest it. I'd been bubbling with confusion and fury, about to lash out, to continue arguing until the doctor saw sense . . . Suddenly I felt limp again, overwhelmed. I feebly waived my hand in Dr. Peters's direction. "I need to be alone for a while. Come back later. I need to . . ."

"Of course."

Relief spread across his face as he gathered his affairs. I heard the click of the door and swivel of the lock. I stared out the window for a long time, seeking some sort of escape from the claustrophobia of my room, perhaps also hoping to catch a glimpse of the woman. I saw nobody. There were bars on the windows. It wasn't that I hadn't noticed them before, I just hadn't paid them any heed. It wasn't so unusual to see bars on a window in New York. Of course it was a good deal stranger to see them on a window many floors up. Too high for a burglar to get in, or indeed for anyone to climb out. They could only be there to stop patients from jumping to their death.

I tried to regulate my breathing. I thought of my aunt and uncle, and the solemn silence of the house they'd brought me up in. They'd since retired to Florida, years ago. I wasn't exactly estranged from them, but I hadn't seen them for a long time and had made no effort to do so. Might they come up to see me? Probably not. My uncle had been unwell for some

time, and it would be a huge undertaking to make the trip.
What did it matter? Dozens of other people right here in New
York would be able to identify me. Thinking it through, trying to calm myself, I began to regain some of my confidence.
There were any number of ways that I could prove who I was,
or, failing that, sow just enough doubt into the doctor's mind
that he'd feel obliged to do something about it—let me call
D'Angelo, for example—if only to cover his back. After all,
I had some unique advantages. I knew how places like this
worked. I knew the kind of things doctors liked to hear. I
knew and could avoid the recognized behavior patterns of
people in the grip of delusion, as I'd seen so many of them.
Given time and persistence on my part, the truth was bound
to come out.

At the same time, I was working through the implications
of what the doctor had revealed. The only way to make sense
of it was that Smith/Esterhazy had died in my bed. The body
had been discovered weeks later, in a state of putrefaction,
and had been mistakenly identified as mine.

There had presumably been a funeral, it occurred to me.
Where? Who had attended? Not my aunt and uncle. My secretary perhaps? D'Angelo? Speelman? Former lovers? The
dozen or so friends with whom I'd kept in sporadic contact?
But who would have told them? They didn't form a network;
they didn't even know each other. One way or another, it
would have been a small affair. Probably an embarrassing one
for all concerned: a clutch of people hoping for it to be over
as quickly as possible. In my mind's eye I surveyed the pro-
ceedings, as if from on high. Was a funeral any sort of way to
mark the end of a life? Even at their best, they seemed such
small things, such a feeble means of summing up something
as astonishing as a human existence. I thought about the memorial service I'd attended as a boy for the tenth anniversary

of the fire that had killed my parents. Afterward, someone had even given me a turn-of-the-century photograph of my father, posed stiffly in a studio, with the luxuriant whiskers and mustache that must have been the fashion back then, but which had looked so otherworldly to me. I'd seen very few pictures of my father, and the effect had been deeply unsettling—all the more so because of the similarities I could detect beneath the facial hair. I remembered people crying at the memorial, consoling themselves, even consoling me. At the time I'd felt a stranger and an impostor among them because I'd never known my parents, and had been sad not because I missed them, but because of the orphan status that their death had bestowed upon me. Now, I felt moved by the memory of this service. My father had been a well-loved figure at the bank that had employed him. My mother, too, had been missed and mourned by the many immigrants to whom she'd given free English lessons at a school in the city. Would anyone have cried at their son's funeral?

A strange thing had happened. The bizarre conversation with the doctor had conjured up another "Dr. Manne" in my mind. I had this image of a shadowy character, born of me and yet not me, stalking me through my life, if indeed it wasn't me who was stalking him through his. It was hard to shake off this disorientating image. And no sooner had I learned of the existence of this "Dr. Manne" than I'd also learned of his death . . . I turned away from the window, and for the thousandth time let my eyes run over the white walls and ceiling.

I'd been so involved in my own private struggle here in the hospital that I hadn't really concerned myself with my disappearance as it would appear to the outside world. I felt a twinge of gratitude toward my secretary for being "distraught" by my "death." Who else would be? My removal from the fabric of New York would go relatively unremarked. I imagined the desultory conversation in some Manhattan bar: "Remember that guy David Manne?" "You mean at med school, the one who married the actress?" "Yeah. Used to run into him every now and then. His office was a block down from mine. Apparently killed himself the other day." "You're joking." "Nope. Can't say I'm too surprised though. Moody guy." How many conversations like that might have taken place? A dozen or so, I guessed. I pictured D'Angelo's wife, as he broke the news to her. Perhaps she'd felt something, a moment of despair, because after all she'd liked me, had seemed to have been attracted to me, even if she'd hardly known me. And then it would be over. After a while, no more bar conversations breaking the news. My apartment would be cleared out and put on the market again, my few possessions disposed of. The new tenant certainly wouldn't be told that the previous one had killed himself there. My office too would be let out, to a proper Park Avenue specialist this time, who'd have to spend good money redecorating the premises before moving in, given the general decline over my ten years' occupancy. Within a matter of months, the city would have smoothed over my death, gotten the wrinkle out; it would be as if it had never happened, as if *I* had never happened.

And life would go on.

4

My relationship with Dr. Peters had moved on. Gone was the relentless questioning and probing of my life story. Now, things were out in the open, the trench lines clearly demarcated. The focus was almost entirely on what in my mind I called the "last days." We would talk about Smith/Esterhazy, my thoughts about the man following me, why he might have wanted to kill me . . . the doctor was gently leading me toward the inconsistencies of my narrative, as if I weren't aware of them. Of course, I knew the strategy from having used it myself, and I played along, taking some sort of pleasure in the duel.

"Tell me," the doctor asked one afternoon, "do you enjoy the movies?"

I shrugged. "I like to go once in a while. Same as anyone else. It's not exactly a passion."

"What kind of movies do you like?"

"I don't know . . ." I was trying to think of one I'd seen recently, or indeed any movie, but my mind was blank.

"What about *Gone With the Wind*?"

"Yes. I've seen that."

"Did you like it?"

"I guess. I don't really remember."

"Not really your cup of tea, though."

"Maybe not."

"What about Jimmy Cagney movies?"

"I've seen a few of those. *The Roaring Twenties*, *The Public Enemy* . . ." Scenes from these came back to me. I could remember them much better than *Gone With the Wind*.

"They're more to your taste."

"Probably."

"What about books? Do you read them?"

"When I was younger I read a lot. The classics. Dickens, Tolstoy, Balzac. These days I don't have the energy for those kinds of books."

"You don't read any more?"

"I do . . . only now, it's dime store stuff. Chandler. Hammett. Maybe Agatha Christie. Books that don't require too much effort."

"I see."

The doctor made notes, seemed to ignore me for a minute or two.

"Why ask me about movies and books? What possible relevance can they have?"

"Has it ever struck you how your story might sound to someone else? Like something from a movie, a thriller. Or a crime novel."

"Maybe. Don't you think your own version of my story is just as far-fetched? Just as much straight out of the movies?"

The moment I said that, I realized something. Of course, in my doctor's eyes, I *was* the perfect patient. The one in a thousand, the case history that could be written up into a true career booster. In which case, it was no longer simply a question of my trying to persuade the doctor of the truth. I'd also have to break down his self-interested resistance. In fact, I'd have to play him like a patient.

"There are two views available to you," the doctor was now saying. "The first is the one you are obstinate in believing. That you were a stooge for some mysterious 'scheme for disappearing people,' to use your own words. That you were tricked into committing a man to a hospital that doesn't exist. That staff at this hospital then let you walk away with him, despite the fact that he was in a state of sedation. That you put him up in your apartment, that he fell into a coma, and shortly after died in your bed. And that for no good reason you've been the victim of a murder attempt. You haven't come up with any sort of coherent picture as to how all this could be true: it's just a string of bizarre fragments. Or there's the other view. That you have suffered something, perhaps a cerebral lesion or some earlier psychic trauma, or a combination of the two, that accounts for your delusional beliefs. Objectively, which do you think the average person would find most likely?"

"If you truly believe I'm deluded, then why on earth are you trying to reason with me? As a psychiatrist, you must know that you can't reason the deluded out of their delusions. You have to find other means."

The doctor went back to scribbling in his pad. I was stupidly pleased with my riposte; something in me was keen to rattle the doctor, over and above any desire to leave the hospital. From a certain perspective, it occurred to me, our roles were interchangeable. Both believing the other to be deluded. Both with a personal stake in convincing the other of his unreason.

"But really. Do I look or act in any way like a drifter from

Ohio? Do I talk like one? Do you even think I have an Ohio accent?"

"Things are learned, unlearned. You've been in New York a decade now. You claim you grew up on Long Island. You don't have a Long Island accent either."

Even as I was speaking, even as I'd brought up the question of accent, I could hear a Midwestern twang creeping into my voice. Similar to the way a wrongly accused man can't help acting guilty, it seemed that if you were treated as a mental patient, you'd ultimately end up behaving like one. Once, in an earlier session, I'd switched off and was in the middle of a daydream when the doctor had suddenly asked me something. Momentarily disoriented, I'd said: "Where am I?" before immediately recognizing it as the kind of thing disturbed patients were always saying out of the blue.

After the doctor had left that day, I felt more unsettled than usual. With this talk of brain lesions and psychic trauma, he'd been blunter than ever before. As if he'd found himself at the end of one strategy, giving it a last shot before embarking on another. It was true that we'd reached some sort of stalemate. By now, I had a reply to just about anything the doctor could throw at me. I had begun to resemble long-term patients I'd known, who'd had all the time in the world to consider and construct an argument against every possible objection to their delusion. It was the irony of mental wards: remove a troubled person from the world, isolate him in a room, and the tendency will always be to go deeper into the delusion, not to pull out of it. Mental asylums bred insanity, just as hospitals bred infection, and prisons criminals.

The stalemate didn't mean that Dr. Peters and I were on an equal footing. Because of the power relation, it actually meant that I was losing. That I would remain incarcerated in the hospital, while the doctor would gain kudos from writing up my case. How could I ever win, when the psychiatric consensus was that denial of the illness was part of the illness? I believed this myself, it was demonstrable, I'd hammered the point home to countless patients. And yet here I was, facing its essential contradiction.

If, as I suspected, the doctor was preparing a new treatment strategy for me, then I could only fear what that might be. Over the years that I'd been practicing psychiatry, I'd found my respect for it slowly ebbing away. Other medical disciplines had grown steadily more empirically based, but psychiatry still seemed like guesswork. It was riddled with invented maladies, with gurus peddling therapies that would become the rage for a while only to prove in time to exacerbate the very conditions they were meant to cure. But these particular gurus were hospital department heads, and if they decided on a certain procedure, then the patient had little to no chance of dodging it.

Some of these pointless therapies I felt I could survive easily enough—the "sleep cure" for instance, or even electrotherapy. But a recently popular one filled me with a peculiar horror. It consisted of first knocking the patient out with an electric shock, then inserting an icepick-like instrument above the patient's eye and scraping it into the frontal lobes. Over the past couple of years I'd seen several of these so-called leucotomized patients. Some had become totally incapacitated, unable to feed or look after themselves. Others were much less badly affected, but they had all possessed the eerie quality of a brain living on as a series of set responses. I'd tried to find out whether these procedures were carried out in the hospital I was in. I'd pressed my ear to the door when I heard doctors and nurses in conversation as they walked by my room; while I was accompanied to the bathroom, I'd scan other patients I passed, on the lookout for the characteristic shuffle of the leucotomized.

The white walls were the polished interior of my own skull—any escape, even if only to a communal room within the hospital, seemed far-fetched. Why couldn't they at least give me books or magazines to read? With so little stimulus, I'd spent inordinate amounts of time staring into the little mirror the nurse had given me. For the first few minutes I'd just accustom myself to my face again. I could still see the ghost of the old one, but that would soon fade and, after a while, I would look relatively normal and natural to myself. That sensation could last quite some time. But always at some point, it would turn. The face would start to seem strange again. It might flicker elusively between normal and alien, but then in the final stage it would cease to look either. It would lose all signification. It wouldn't be a face at all. Just a collection of lines, curves, colors, contours.

For want of anything better to do, I picked up the pages I'd written about Abby. I'd had a notion to write more, and glanced briefly at what I'd already done. The sentences and thoughts seemed disjointed now, although they had not appeared like that when I'd written them. That story about the friend who'd drowned in the lake: it was a shock to realize that I'd gotten it quite wrong. It hadn't been Abby who'd told me about that at all. It had been a patient, Miss Fregoli. The one who had later committed suicide. It shook me that I could make a mistake like that.

My thoughts drifted from Abby to Miss Fregoli then back to Abby again. I remembered the moment I'd known she'd been unfaithful to me. A letter in the morning mail, which wouldn't have aroused any suspicion if she hadn't hurriedly put it in her bag without even opening it. Even then I hadn't realized, it had only hit me with full force an hour later, in the subway, while reading about a case of adultery and murder in the *Times*. Suddenly everything had felt flat, devoid of emotional substance, slowed down. I'd once been knocked down by a car on Park Avenue: this felt the same. If I'd gone back and confronted Abby there and then, she would have told me the truth. Instead I'd let it fester. I'd followed her one day and seen her with Speelman, walking arm in arm, talking gaily, barely aware of the world around them. It was as if I'd opened the door to their bedroom.

I tried to imagine her last days. It occurred to me that if she'd had a tumor removed from her trachea, she probably wouldn't have been able to speak. She'd have been rendered mute. "Yours was the kind of ambition that meant at some point stepping into a void," I now found myself writing. "With me it was quite different. I'd work methodically, without the possibility of error, until I'd gotten to where I thought I wanted to be." I stopped, and knew instinctively that if I looked up now, I'd see the woman from across the courtyard. Once again I felt she was staring directly at me, although at this distance her eyes were merely two black points. I felt compelled to get off my bed and walk across the room to the window. I opened it and put my hands to the bars. At the same time I was wondering, for the first time, who had been here in this room before me. Whoever he was, he too had probably spent hours staring out this window. Had he seen the woman? Had she stared back? I thought I saw her slightly shake her head and then, more obviously, raise her hands in an almost supplicatory manner. It wasn't clear to me what she'd meant with the gesture, if she'd meant anything at all, but I couldn't help feeling that it was directed at me. There

was a presence between us, a ghost. It was "Dr. Manne." But
he had withered to almost nothing. He was someone without
potential, without a future, not a person at all, since people
live in their future. I turned away and sat back on my bed,
once again locked into the absolute solitude I'd always feared
and desired.

5

"He's coming back to me."

"Who is?"

"Stephen Smith. He's been coming back to me. All night."

"Tell me about him."

"You were right. He comes from Ohio. He doesn't miss it. Sometimes he misses the feeling of space."

"Who are his parents?"

"I don't know. I think his mother died. When he was very young. His father might be alive. There was a meeting, when he was a child. His Dad was drunk."

"Who raised him?"

"Foster parents. Kind people. In the end, it wasn't enough."

"Why did he leave?"

"Trouble with the law. Nothing too serious. He'd been caught once and let go. But was told it'd be jail next time. He jumped a train and knew he'd never be back."

"Tell me more. Tell me about New York."

"New York was tough. The thieving wasn't easy. I tried my

hand at pickpocketing. In the stations and subway. I was no good at it."

"What did you do next?"

"I kept at it. But there were other pickpockets. Gangs of them, guarding their patch. One day they chased me, bashed me half to death."

"Bashed you unconscious?"

"Yes. I woke up by the docks. A kind gentleman took me to a hospital. They bandaged me up."

"What happened next?"

"The gentleman got me cleaned up and bought me lunch."

"What was his name?"

"Esterhazy."

"Did you stay in touch with him?"

"No. Years later, I thought I saw him in the street. I followed him for a block or two. Because after buying me lunch that day, he'd given me money. And I'd wanted to pay him back. But when I finally caught up with the man, it turned out to be someone else. It wasn't Esterhazy after all."

"After the hospital, what did you do?"

"I had the money. It was spring. I figured if I slept in the park, the money might last me a few weeks. Long enough for me to get better."

"And that's what you did."

"Yes. But it was never the same, after the bashing."

"In what way?"

"The headaches. I couldn't concentrate so well. I'd lose my temper."

"Did you work?"

"I got jobs, down by the docks. They never lasted long."

"Where did you live?"

"I moved around. Cheap hotels. Friends' places. Parks."

"Did you ever go back to hospital?"

"Once, yes."

"Tell me about it."

"I don't want to."

"Why not?"

"It pains me to think of it."

"Are you Stephen Smith?"

"I'm David Manne."

"Are you Stephen Smith?"

"No."

"Are you Stephen Smith?"

"I'm tired. I haven't slept. Please leave me now."

The squeak of the linoleum, the door opening and closing, the turn of the key: I was alone again. It was true what I'd said about being tired. Just talking to the doctor had exhausted me, although it had been no effort at all to come up with the story of Stephen Smith. On the contrary, the details had flowed out of me, almost of their own accord. Of course, I now realized, I'd drawn on past case histories of patients of mine, so many of whom had spent time as a vagrant. On top of the tiredness, or because of it, I could feel the kick of euphoria. I could have easily botched it. Instead, my performance had seemed real enough, to me at least. I knew I had to pay attention. It was common enough for patients to fake it, to humor their doctor, for whatever reason. A good psychiatrist would view any surrender with suspicion. In the coming days and weeks, I could look forward to continued probing from Dr. Peters. I'd have to carefully construct my capitulation.

There was something else to the euphoria as well. Once I'd finally decided to ditch Manne, I'd felt liberated. And Smith had mysteriously come to life. I'd sensed it even before the doctor had entered the room. It wasn't only that Stephen Smith was now my best chance of getting out. I'd begun to have hopes for him. After all, he was starting from nowhere.

He was someone who could still invent himself, begin afresh. On the face of it, Manne had a lot more going for him. Manne was educated, a professional; Smith was a homeless man, with a history of mental instability and suicide attempts. But Manne had made choices that had remorselessly narrowed his horizons, until finally they'd vanished altogether. For Manne, there could be no real continuation, except in a sort of living death.

"Tell me about David Manne."

"I don't know anything about him."

"Are you David Manne?"

"No. I'm Stephen Smith."

"Who is David Manne?"

"I don't know."

"Then tell me about someone you do know."

"Like who?"

"Like the photo. On your bedside table. Who is she?"

"Her name is Marie."

"Tell me about her."

"Marie? She was a few years older than me. It was after the war. The refugee boats were coming in. Down by the docks there were two big warehouses converted into dormitories. One for men, one for women and children. Refugees could stay there free, for a week. I was working at the Coimbra Shipping office opposite."

"She was a refugee?"

"Yes."

"How did you meet?"

"I came across her, sitting on a suitcase in the street. She'd spent her week in the dormitory. After, she had nowhere to go."

"What did you do?"

"I bought her a cup of coffee. Then I found her somewhere to stay for a few nights."

"Did you see her again?"

"I took her to the movies one night. She didn't talk about herself. After, I asked her if she wanted to get a drink. I took her to bed, in my room at a boarding house."

"Was that the only time?"

"No. We wound up living together for a while. She had a husband in Europe. She didn't know whether he was dead or alive. So we pretended to be married. We rented two rooms in a street near the docks. For a while we were happy. Then I started imagining things. One night I threatened her with a broken bottle. She called the police."

"What did they do?"

"They restrained me. They got a doctor. He committed me."

"What was the doctor's name?"

"I don't know."

"Could it have been Manne?"

"I don't know."

"Was it Manne?"

"No."

"It was Manne, wasn't it?"

The woman on the balcony disappeared. Perhaps she'd moved out, perhaps she'd taken a vacation, perhaps it was too cold to stand on the balcony any more. But I couldn't help thinking that it was because of me. She'd vanished at the very moment I'd given Manne up—I felt the connection even if I couldn't see what it might be. A week at least had gone by, and although my hopes of seeing her again diminished with each day, it didn't stop me from looking out the window. But after a while, it started to feel right that she was no longer there. I saw that final supplicatory gesture of hers as a sort of goodbye.

I was astonished to have a visitor one day. His name was
Peter Untermeyer, and he'd been a psychiatry intern with me
at Bellevue, years ago. I'd only seen him once since, a chance
meeting in the street. He'd been in uniform, I now remembered, and was just back from Europe. I'd asked him what
he was up to and he'd told me about a psychiatric unit he
was helping to set up. We're looking for people right now,
he'd said, doctors and psychiatrists to join the team. Perhaps
I might be interested? I'd followed him to an office in a ram-
shackle building in Turtle Bay, on one of the streets they'd
later razed for the UN headquarters. He'd been all apologetic
about the premises and had said they'd soon be moving uptown, now that the army funding had come through. After
introducing me to a few of his colleagues there, he'd outlined
some crackpot psychiatric model they were working on, the
details of which I could no longer recall. I remembered saying I'd think about it, that I'd call, although I never had—at
that time I'd still entertained hopes for my Park Avenue career. And that had been the last time I'd had anything to do
with him.

Why on earth was Untermeyer here in front of me now?
He was asking me questions about Stephen Smith, and I was
blankly regurgitating what I'd already recounted to the doctor. He was looking straight into my eyes, seemingly without
a flicker of recognition. Could he really not see who I was?
Had I changed so much? I let the Stephen Smith persona
ramble on, while I tried to pull together an idea of what could
have led Untermeyer here. Perhaps he was already working in
the hospital. Perhaps he'd heard the story of a patient supposedly impersonating someone he vaguely remembered from
student days. Intrigued, he'd asked Dr. Peters if he could see
the patient . . . But I couldn't quite make that story stand. Yes,
he might not recognize me had he not been expecting to see

me. After all, I myself might not have recognized Untermeyer had I simply crossed by him in the corridor. But a one-on-one meeting with the background I'd just dreamed up—no, it was impossible, regardless of how much I'd changed.

As he took leave of me, I searched his face for some hint of double play. But I could see nothing in that smooth expanse, no sense of the mind behind it. For a moment I considered blurting out: "Don't you remember me? Can't you see who I really am?" But I held back. Even if I couldn't piece together why, I had this feeling that Untermeyer's appearance was some kind of trick. Perhaps a sly means of getting me to admit that I didn't really believe in Stephen Smith.

Sitting on my bed, staring at the door that Untermeyer had just closed, I realized that if I were to persuade the doctor that I wasn't shamming, then I'd have to go some way toward persuading myself as well. I had to mourn the death of Manne, while at the same time assist in the birth of Smith. Right now, the two felt equally distant from me. Equally unreal. I was located somehow in a void between them, observing both as if they were someone else.

Then I'd find myself turning inward. And I'd search. And there was nothing.

"David Manne."

"What of him?"

"Who was he? Tell me about him."

"He was my doctor. He visited me in the hospital. One day he came to discharge me. They didn't want him to. There'd been an argument. Finally I was allowed out, on condition that I saw Dr. Manne once a week."

"Which was what you did?"

"For a time, yes."

"How did you learn so much about him?"

"We met on Friday afternoons. One day, he let slip that mine was his last appointment of the week. Afterward, I waited outside and saw him come out of the building. I followed him into the subway and home. So now I knew where he lived."

"What did you do then?"

"I came back the next morning. I waited at the corner. I'd only been there a few minutes when I saw him come out again. He went to a diner across the street. He ordered eggs, bacon, toast, coffee. Later, I learned that he ordered the same thing at the same diner, every day. Anyway, he finished his breakfast, paid the check, and left. And I followed him."

"Why?"

"I wanted to know who he was. How he passed his time. He knew everything about me, but I knew nothing about him. I thought it was only fair."

"So what did he do?"

"Nothing special. He bought a newspaper. He went walking in the Park. Later on he took a subway downtown. He wandered around the Village for a while and stopped for lunch. He did some window-shopping and bought a book at a secondhand bookstore. He took the subway back uptown, went to another diner, read his book over dinner. Then he went back home."

"How often did you follow him?"

"Every weekend. But it was mostly the same. Breakfast, a walk in the Park, a little window-shopping or maybe a museum or gallery. It never varied much."

"Did he ever meet anyone?"

"Sometimes. There were young women. I remember one occasion. He'd gone into a phone booth and made a call. Which surprised me, because he'd never done that before.

Afterward, he'd ridden the subway up to the West Eighties or
Nineties. He'd gone to a bar where a woman was waiting for
him, in a booth by the window. She was young, well dressed,
although not especially beautiful. At first they'd both seemed
uneasy, embarrassed. But as time passed I could see them re-
laxing, leaning into each other. I watched them as they talked
nonstop for about an hour. Eventually, it was time to go. He
paid and then they were on the sidewalk, still talking, but I
couldn't catch what they were saying. I could just hear the
tone of the voices, which sounded melancholy. Things were
winding up. They were making the goodbye gestures. She
kind of pecked him on the cheek. There was a pause, as if
they both knew something else was needed. Then he almost
lunged at her. They were in each other's arms for a good minute or so. After that she walked off, without looking back.
Manne just stood there for quite a while. I thought I could see
tears on his cheeks but I wasn't sure. He was badly shaken up,
though, I was sure enough of that. He wandered back down
into the subway, but I didn't follow. Instead I went off in the
other direction. I knew I had to find out who the woman was."

"And did you?"

"Not then. But later, yes. She was Abby Speelman, Manne's
former wife."

I couldn't stop puzzling over the Untermeyer visit. No scenario I came up with really explained it. There was that odd
coincidence: on the night in my apartment with Esterhazy
in my bed, I had thought of Untermeyer, for the first time in
years. I'd wondered whether the psychiatric unit he'd been
setting up had had something to do with the Stevens Institute.
And yet why on earth should I have been wondering that?
Why should I have dragged up from my memory a chance

meeting from long ago? I reflected upon this conundrum on and off for days. Why should Untermeyer have sprung to mind, and how was that connected with his subsequent reappearance? But wasn't this exactly the kind of coincidence that the deluded always fixated upon? Once more, the trouble of having no outside reference points, no guiding stars. The awful necessity of recreating the world from your own mind. At the same time, your sense of self diminishes, dissipated into the very world you've created.

Perhaps Dr. Peters *didn't* actually believe I was Stephen Smith. My supposed suicide attempt, my "paranoid" beliefs, my seemingly bizarre behavior had all led to my being sent to a mental ward after the accident, but the "Stephen Smith" story was some new kind of therapy. A means of resolving personality problems at a remove, through the creation of a different persona . . . I'd vaguely heard of such a therapy, through journal articles I'd skimmed over. As thoroughly unlikely as this scenario was, it at least had the merit of making sense of the Untermeyer visit. He'd have known my identity, but had simply refrained from saying so. If this were the case, how should I now proceed? I sat there musing and losing myself down myriad paths of reasoning and fantasy for what seemed like hours, without ever coming to any firm conclusions.

"You once described to me the interior of Dr. Manne's apartment. Your description matched the photos I was shown in the police file. You told me Manne had a gramophone player, and that he liked Beethoven. Gramophone recordings of Beethoven sonatas were found in his apartment. How did you know these things?"

"It's not hard to guess the layout of a Manhattan apart-

ment. As for Beethoven, I have no idea. He must have told
me himself."

"Did he tell you about the painting on his bedroom wall?
The bottle of whiskey in the cupboard?"

"I suppose he must have."

"Have you ever been in Manne's apartment?"

"No."

"You've never been in Manne's apartment."

"No. Does it matter?"

"You've been there. I know. Why don't you tell me about it?"

"All right . . . if it means so much to you. One day I followed
Manne from only four or five paces behind. I don't know why.
Perhaps I'd actually wanted him to turn around and see me.
He never did. When he finally went back home, I'd sneaked
into the building behind him. I waited at the bottom of the
stairs as he climbed up to the second floor. I could hear him
fumbling around in his pockets for his keys, and not finding
them. He'd left them somewhere, or had maybe accidently
shut them inside. I quietly climbed up a little until I could see
him. Now he was crouched down, halfway up the next flight
of stairs. He took a key from under the carpet, then went back
to his door and opened it. So now I knew where he kept his
spare key."

"And you used it?"

"Yes. That was a Sunday. The next morning I waited until
Manne had left for his office. I got into his building and dug
out the key from under the carpet. I opened his front door
and walked in. It was a weird thrill to be there. The apartment was stark and bare, just how I'd imagined it. His bed was
neatly made, I noticed, whereas I rarely made mine, unless I
was sleeping with someone. On the wall was a large portrait of
a nude. I wondered whether it was Manne's former wife, but I
wasn't sure. She was pictured standing in a doorway, looking

through to a room you couldn't see, and perhaps to another
person there. It seemed to capture the moment before or after
something. The eroticism was at odds with the severity of the
rest of the apartment, and gave me a new sense of who Manne
might be. For a second I had the impression that the room the
woman was looking into was real, that I might go through
the canvas and discover its secrets myself. I walked back to
the front room, then through to a tiny kitchen, maybe to escape the picture. There was a cupboard. In it I found a half-
empty bottle of whiskey, and poured some into a tumbler. I
opened a drawer. A pack of cigarettes was shoved down the
back. I pulled one out. I lit it with a book of matches that had
the name "Le Zinc" printed on its cover. Under that was an
address I knew, a place I drank at in the East Fifties, not far
from Manne's apartment. It wasn't called Le Zinc, though. It
was Albert's Bar & Grill. Perhaps I was mistaken. But I knew
the street well, since I'd once worked there, and there was
nothing called Le Zinc on it. I pondered that for a moment.
I'd had no breakfast, and the whiskey was going to my head.
I went back to the sitting room. In the corner was a gramophone player, with a dozen or so records stacked up against
it. I pulled one out at random, cranked up the player and put
it on. A mournful piano piece barely broke through the clicks
and scratches. It added to my sense of foreboding. I didn't
know why I'd put it on, because I've never liked gramophone
recordings. There's something ghostly about them. I stood
there feeling transfigured, as if in a scene or a photograph.
The apartment was no projection of Manne, it *was* Manne.
The painting of the nude, the whiskey, the matchbook, the
music, the scratches of a record that had been played a thousand times before. The special intimacy of a room seen and
lived in by one person only. I threw up my hands in front of
me and felt I barely recognized them. I resisted the desire to

look at myself in the mirror. I pushed my hands back into my pockets as if to banish them from sight. I could feel my lucky coin in my left pocket. It had been given to me by a Portuguese sailor, for the drink I'd bought him. I pulled it out and placed it on Manne's table. And then I left."

6

Perhaps I'd passed some kind of test, because soon after Untermeyer's visit I was allowed into the communal room. The scene there was familiar to me from my time as a psychiatric intern, even if I was now seeing it all from the other side of the looking glass. The dozen or so men sunk deep into shabby armchairs, dozing or staring at the garish wallpaper; a few more playing a desultory game of cards around a green table; others absorbed in their often eccentric hobbies; the dirty net curtains hanging over the barred windows. I recognized the different types of patient, too—an arc that stretched from the newcomer (anxious, nervy, solitary) to the regular (more vocal, sociable, highly sensitive to status), then finally to the old-timer, who'd slipped into a deathly routine from which he would now never be shaken. I was surprised at how easily I slotted into this scheme of things: how I too would sink into my armchair, refusing to meet the eyes of the others or enter into conversation with them.

Occasionally I'd glance through one of the magazines

lying about, invariably an ancient copy of *Life* or *Look*, never anything remotely current. The radio, too, would warble old show tunes from before the war, forever shrouding the patients in a forgetful nostalgia. On the walls were faded pictures of New York landmarks—the Empire State Building, Brooklyn Bridge, Central Park—like images from a collective dream. A large map of New York hung above the mantelpiece. When the mood struck me, I could spend hours staring at it, daydreaming about places I'd been to or tracing out past journeys. Living in Manhattan, I'd sometimes found its grid-like cityscape oppressive, but now I marveled at the simplicity and perfection. In my state of incarceration, it seemed to me that the map was real and the city a mere abstraction of it. There was a shiny blank spot in the midtown area, not far from where my old apartment was—the ink had rubbed off because so many people had put their finger there. It was no doubt where we were located. I'd always assumed we were somewhere downtown. I knew all the psychiatric hospitals in Manhattan, and could think of none where this was supposed to be. It was a shock to realize how close I was to where I used to live. In my mind, the hospital and the apartment were almost metaphysically different worlds. They couldn't possibly be only twenty minutes' walk from each other.

I noticed the slurring speech and shuffling gait of a couple of the inmates. It might have been early onset dementia— common enough among middle-aged psychiatric patients— or any number of other things. But I knew it was evidence of leucotomy. The procedures could have been done in another hospital, but why not right here? Perhaps they'd already done it to me. After all, the doctor would never tell the patient about the leucotomy, either before or after. The patient was of course aware that *something* had been done to him, but not what. In my case, such a procedure could have been carried out while I was anaesthetized, and they were taking the staples out of my head. Objectively, how could I tell? Perhaps it was consistent with this vacuum I now felt inside me, this sense of being no one or anyone.

A privilege of the "communal" patients was that they were allowed to receive mail. That, too, marked out the different categories of patients. The newcomers would be desperately keen to receive their letters, and nervy if the mailman was late or there was nothing for them that day. The regulars were more ambivalent; they didn't jump up and pester the mailman like the newcomers, they patiently waited until he came around to them. But the old-timers were indifferent to the whole ritual. They got fewer letters than the others, and more often than not left them on the table unopened for the nurses to collect when they returned to their rooms. It was easy enough to understand why. For them, the outside world had simply ceased to exist. It had been squeezed out by the intense life of the mind peculiar to the psychiatric ward.

"Stephen Smith? Letter for you."

"Couldn't be. No one knows I'm here."

"Take a look for yourself, bud."

The name was carefully printed on the envelope, which had already been opened. I pulled out a single sheet of paper. The uncertain scrawl was hard to make out:

Dear Son,

They tell me your being treated in a hospital and I can write you there. I hope you recover from whatever ails you. Son, I know I been a no good father to you. I remember when you was a baby. I remember when you was a little boy and it brings tears to my eyes. I know you have had troubles. If

your ever tiring of life in the city, you have a home
right here in Somerville. I live out here with my new
wife and her son. There is a bed for you.

Your Loving Father

I put the letter down on the table by my armchair, then
shoved it between the pages of a magazine. My hand was
trembling as I did it, and I was also repeatedly shaking my
head—a tic I seemed to have picked up from the other patients. I stared at the map of New York again, before shut-
ting my eyes. I knew the layout of the city better now than I
ever had when I'd actually walked its streets; I could visual-
ize its avenues, subway stations, parks, districts. I fixated on
the blank spot where the ink had rubbed off, and entertained
a whimsy that the corresponding area in Manhattan might
have disappeared as well.

In another part of my mind, though, I was working out
the implications of the letter I'd received. The hospital people,
or perhaps the police, had tracked down Smith's father and,
who knows, perhaps other members of his family. The letter did nothing to contradict the story I'd given the doctor.
If anything, it confirmed it too well. What were the chances
that Smith's father might turn up in New York? Minimal, I
supposed, given that the man was a barely literate alcoholic.
I pulled myself up short: how did I know he was alcoholic?
That was only a colorful bit of gloss I'd given Dr. Peters. Nonetheless, it felt true. Absurdly, the letter had moved me greatly,
had almost brought me to tears, and another corner of my
mind had conjured up a silly fantasy. What if I replied to the
letter, taking the man up on his offer to stay with him and
his wife? Perhaps it would be my ticket out of here. I'd be living in a family, as part of a family, something I'd never really

experienced. It might give me that emotional anchor I'd always lacked. My father had mentioned a stepson. Perhaps I could be an older brother to the boy, a mentor, which would give some shape to my own life. After all, my father had had his second shot at life. He'd remarried, moved to a new town. Why couldn't I do the same?

I shook this ridiculous fantasy from my mind. At the same time, a new idea had taken root. Maybe this letter wasn't real at all. Dr. Peters had fabricated it as some kind of trick or test, to see how I'd react. I worked my way back from this premise, trying to see why it might be true and how it might play out. But the line of thought quickly fizzled to nothing. It was too easy to get lost in speculation, with such a slender thread to follow. Too easy to succumb to the paranoia of the psychiatric ward, so contagious that even the doctors and nurses ended up infected by it.

A pudgy-faced, corpulent man tapped me on the shoulder: "Remember me?"

I scrutinized his features. For a moment I thought he might be an old patient of mine: the possibility of bumping into one here was something that had haunted me.

"No, I don't."

"You're Smith, aren't you?"

"That's right."

"We worked together a few years ago. On the waterfront. Coimbra Shipping Company."

"I . . . yes, I remember the job, don't remember you."

"Well, I'll be . . . Guess I must have changed, even more than I thought. You really don't know who I am?"

"I really don't."

"We used to go out drinking together. Say, whatever happened to that girl you were seeing? The foreign one? Pretty little thing."

"She . . . she . . . we stopped seeing each other. I don't know what happened to her."

"I just can't believe you don't remember me. Torma. Joe Torma. We shared a flophouse room. On the Bowery. For a good month or so. You must remember that."

"Yes. I remember that. I remember Joe Torma. You've put on weight. You look different. That's all."

"You had a fight with the boss, didn't you? And then you took off. That's the last I heard of you. What happened? How'd you smash up your face like that?"

"Things got bad. You know, same old story. Couldn't find work, lost my girl. Couldn't see a way ahead. Ended up throwing myself on the rails. Somehow I survived and they put me here . . . What about you?"

"Me? I stayed with the Coimbra people. Then one day I got slammed in the head with some timber we were loading. Fished out of the river and out cold for hours, so they tell me. Been in and out of hospitals ever since. I'm getting better though. I'll be outta here soon. I'll be back at work."

I looked him over. One shoulder was slightly lower than the other, and so was one side of his face. He spoke hesitantly, out of the corner of his mouth. It wasn't easy to understand what he was saying, and he seemed to have trouble saying it. All quite consistent with some severe craniocerebral trauma. I doubted he'd be back at work, not soon, not ever. In fact, I could already map out the rest of his existence, based on the life stories of patients I'd had. If lucky, they'd let him stay here in the hospital, which didn't seem such a bad place, all things considered. But probably they'd let him go at some point. Without any support, he'd last a year or two on the streets at most. Or perhaps he had family to look after him, and then it would be longer. He wouldn't be able to hold down a job, and he'd end up sitting at home all day listening to the radio. He might take to drink. His personality would start to change. He'd become disinhibited, angry, violent, too fresh with the girls. Consequently he'd be increasingly left alone, which would only exacerbate the symptoms. He was perhaps around thirty now, and the serious decline would set in in around five years' time. He'd be dead by forty, of a seizure, stroke, alcohol poisoning, or something else.

"Good luck, Joe. I'm sure you'll be out soon."

"Thanks. And good luck to you too."

He loped over to one of the other armchairs. Strange how they were all arranged in a semicircle around the fireplace, even though it had clearly long been boarded up and wall-papered over. I watched him from a distance. Joe Torma. I knew no one of that name. He'd mistaken me for some other Smith—not exactly an uncommon surname. Or else, it was another of Dr. Peters's ruses. He'd briefed Torma, asked him to pretend he knew me, as part of my ongoing treatment. There was that line about the Coimbra Shipping Company. Hadn't I come up with something like that for Dr. Peters? There were times when it felt like I'd interiorized the doctor, that he was somehow observing me from the inside.

It was midafternoon. Torma was now dozing in his armchair. I rose from mine, and walked over to the window. The view was the same as from my room, only we were three floors below. Down in the courtyard there was an annex with a glass roof—it housed a printing press, one of the other patients had told me. The bright winter sunlight bounced off the roof, dazzling me. If I shaded my eyes a little, I could see the tiny reflection of myself in the glass down below, haloed by white light. I'd heard of a gruesome tragedy that had taken place here, a few years back. A patient had somehow gotten the bar frame off and jumped out, crashing through the glass below and impaling himself on a machine lever.

If I craned my head at a certain angle and looked up, I could just about see the balcony opposite my own room. Something was fluttering above the ledge. Was the woman out there? Difficult to tell, but I suddenly felt certain that she was. I moved away from the window, then made my way out of the communal room and up the stairs. If you left before the bell, you were supposed to tell the nurse in charge, and I'd probably get in trouble for not doing so, but I wasn't thinking about that. Instead I was replaying in my mind a dream I'd recently had. I was in her apartment. I could see it all precisely, with a most undreamlike lucidity: the portrait on the wall, the corner kitchen with the icebox, the door through to the bedroom, the bed on which she lay. I was getting undressed, excited. She was waiting for me, I was eager to join her. At the same time, I'd felt an urge to go out on the balcony first. I stood there naked. Across the courtyard was the small window. I strained to make out the blurry figure staring through the bars.

Now I was walking along the corridor to my room. Just as I was about to go in, I heard a muffled thump that seemed to come from inside. It was as though someone had lightly banged the wall with his fist. A sense of unease invaded me, and I waited for a moment outside the door, but I couldn't hear anything else. I turned the handle slowly. The room was cloaked in a gray light. I noticed a mark on the wall that I didn't think had been there before. My notebook was on the floor. There was some white substance on the chair. I felt the presence of something, even before I saw it.

A small bird, a swallow I thought, lay on my bed, one wing tucked to its body, the other unfurled. Its head was cocked in my direction. I could see its eyes swivel as I moved into the room. Other patients would leave breadcrumbs for the birds on their windowsills, but I'd never done that. How had it gotten in here? The window was firmly shut, just as I'd left it. Perhaps the nurse or cleaner had been in while I'd been downstairs. Perhaps she'd opened the window to air the room, then closed it upon leaving, without noticing that a bird had flown in. Not a very likely story, but I could think of no better one.

I watched the bird for several minutes. I imagined it flying in, suddenly finding itself in a closed world of alien geometry, then rushing at the window only to hit solid air. I imagined it flapping about desperately, dashing itself against the walls, until it dropped back exhausted onto the bed. I approached slowly, so as not to frighten it. I stretched my hand toward it, and cupped it gently off the bed. The bird offered no resistance. I could see and feel the palpitations of its tiny breast. Its eyes were dilated. I tucked the unfurled wing back to its body. Its head was pressed against my palm. I didn't know whether it was injured or not, whether it would fly back out toward the light or fall helplessly to the glass roof. I looked through the bars to the balcony opposite, but to my surprise there was no one there.

I opened the window. Then I opened my hand.

PART THREE

I

It felt like midtown Manhattan, and the street signs confirmed that it was, but I didn't recognize any of the buildings or landmarks. Odd, because this was a part of town that in theory I knew well. It was as if all the specifics had been stripped out, and I'd found myself in a generic version of the neighborhood. But after wandering about in a state of bewilderment for an hour or so, I turned a corner and it was like I'd crossed a boundary. I knew where I was again. I was back in my old life. There was the bakery where I sometimes bought doughnuts. The place where I got my shoes resoled. The hawker who sold me the *Times*. If anything, the street was too familiar, a vast simulacrum that had been waiting there for me to find it.

I was in sight of my apartment building, staring down at me from the other side of the intersection. The courtyard was through a gate, and then up the stairs was my door. The spare key I'd hidden under the carpet in the stairwell was no doubt still there. I imagined unlocking the door and walking through to the front room. Everything would be the same,

everything different. The records stacked against the gramophone player; the empty whiskey bottle; the novel opened
face down on the table. The phone would ring. It would be
the girl I'd flirted with over the summer, inviting me out for
a drink. Or my secretary, with another appointment to add
to my schedule. I'd speak briefly then put down the receiver.
In the bedroom, the woman in the doorway was turned away
from me, staring into another room that wasn't there. I'd open
the wardrobe that constituted an entire wall. Inside, a row of
identical suits, shirts, ties. I'd change clothes and walk back
out of the apartment, slamming the door behind me.

Why shouldn't I be able to slip back into my former life
like that? To do so would be no more extraordinary than the
way I'd slipped out of it. I crossed the street. At closer range,
I could see that the building wasn't quite as it used to be. It
was shabbier. The apartments that looked onto the street were
now unoccupied. On the fourth floor, a window was broken.
Even while I'd been living there, the block had been gradually
emptying out. Presumably the owner wasn't renewing leases;
he probably wanted to redevelop the property. During my ten
years in this neighborhood there'd been dramatic changes,
as old tenement buildings had been torn down or remodeled
into luxury residences. An uneasy superimposition of two
worlds now existed; in some streets only a wall separated the
super-wealthy from the families on relief in their cold-water
walk-ups.

I'd fully intended to go into the building, but instead
found myself walking right past it. At the end of the block
was the diner I'd always breakfasted at, every weekend and
most weekdays too. It had also changed, but I couldn't really
pinpoint how. Rather, I was the one who had changed, which
had the effect of making strange what had been familiar. I
sat down at my usual table. Next to me was a man I'd seen

there a hundred times—an insurance executive who lived on Sutton Place and was separated from his wife. There were a dozen other details I knew about him from overheard conversations. But if he were at all surprised to see me there, he didn't show it.

"Two eggs over easy, bacon, toast, coffee, please."

"Coming right up."

The waitress gave the tabletop a cursory wipe, shouted the order through the swinging doors, then moved on to the insurance man. Not a flicker of recognition. And yet she'd *have* to recognize me, even with my injuries. And it would *have* to be surprising. There would have been street gossip, surely she'd have heard about what had happened to Manne. Even if she hadn't, I was a regular of a decade's standing who had suddenly reappeared, months after suddenly disappearing. I couldn't rid myself of this feeling that she—along with the other regulars who were paying me no heed—was simply playing a role. Her face was a mask, she wasn't entirely real. But hadn't I always had that vague impression? I tried to rationalize the waitress's nonreaction. We'd always performed an awkward pantomime, in which she'd pretend she didn't know what I was about to order, although I'd always have the same thing every day. Perhaps she was consciously, or subconsciously, playing a version of the same game.

Sipping my coffee, musing on all this, I happened to glimpse my reflection in a mirror behind the bar. It was always a peculiar sensation, when you caught yourself unawares like that. You had the momentary impression of seeing someone else, before the jolting realization that it was actually you. This time the initial effect lasted even longer than usual. The hospital had given me a cheap, ill-fitting suit—probably from a deceased estate—and I'd also bought a secondhand fedora from a dime store, to pull down low over my scarred face. In short, I looked nothing like Manne. But I did look a lot like Smith. Perhaps it wasn't so strange that the waitress hadn't recognized me. A regular patient had once accosted me in the street and I simply hadn't realized who he was, out of the context of my office.

I ate quickly, paid up, and left. No point in hanging around. The trace of Manne's existence ran like a seam through this neighborhood, but I had no desire to stake my claims on him. If I were spooked by no one recognizing me, I'd surely be even more so if someone did. Back on the sidewalk, I wandered on, taking random turns until I was less familiar with the terrain. The jostling mass of people unnerved me. In the hospital, my life had slowed to a point where it had practically stopped, whereas here on the street, everything was a blur of incomprehensible movement, the present moment reduced to an infinitely small point. Where could all these people be heading, with such blank determination? No one looked at me; some looked through me. After the months of intense one-on-one meetings with the doctor, with all my bodily needs seen to by hospital staff, it felt bizarre to be so comprehensively ignored.

A subway sign was up ahead. I took out a piece of paper with the address of the hotel I'd been booked into. Somewhere way downtown—Smith territory, no doubt. I found myself going down the subway steps. It wasn't the same station I'd last been in, but it was fitted out as to be almost indistinguishable, apart from the name. Before leaving the hospital, I'd wondered whether I might develop a phobia about the subway. It didn't seem to be the case, although standing on the platform I kept well away from the rails. Manne's last few seconds replayed in my mind, without my being able to stop the scene, or even wanting to. I could see him making his way through the crowd onto the platform; behind him, a shadowy figure I couldn't quite make out, just the shape of his hand as he gave Manne a violent shove. Even then, Manne had almost managed to maintain his balance, and there was a moment when he might have been able to regain the platform, had anyone helped, or perhaps had he really wanted to. There he remained, frozen a moment before his descent, one foot still on the edge of the platform, the other in space. I wasn't Manne, I was a simple bystander. A woman beside me had put her shopping bag down by her feet; it was half-open, and she'd carelessly thrown her purse on top. On my other side a man had his back to me, his wallet visibly bulging through his pocket. You could probably make a decent living pickpocketing here, it struck me as the train sidled into the station.

They'd booked me a room in one of those scrappy Third Avenue hotels for itinerant workers. The woman at the desk handed me the key: "You're okay 'til the end of the month. You can stay on after, so long as you pay upfront and you're no trouble." I climbed the three flights of stairs and opened the door to my new home. Inside, a bed, table and chair, bare white walls. Not so different from my hospital room, although in worse repair. There was even a window looking onto a courtyard. I walked over and stared out. No balcony opposite, no woman standing there. Just a brick wall.

It was a relief to close the door and shut the world out: the big-city crowds would take some getting used to. I lay down on my bed and stared at the ceiling with my hands behind my head, just as I'd done for hours on end in the hospital— I couldn't quite stop myself vaguely expecting the nurse or doctor to appear at the door at any moment. I was on my own now, though. In my mind I ran through the events of the day, but in a detached kind of way. Manne remained an enigma to me, but one I no longer needed to understand. The events that had ended in my committal—the Esterhazy case, the Stevens Institute, the subway incident—were like a meta-physical knot tied through the middle of my life, separating it into two discrete experiences. I might now never undo this knot. The past was irretrievable, even through memory. It was haunting, painful, strange like a dream. The present, and the foreseeable future as well, were Smith's domain.

Tomorrow, I'd start at the job they'd fixed up for me, down by the Chelsea Piers.

2

Manne had been a voracious reader of newspapers. Smith rarely looked at them. But one afternoon I noticed a newsstand headline about a city fire. The day before I'd seen plumes of smoke rising above the skyline to the north as we'd unloaded a company ship. I bought the evening paper for a change and read about the huge blaze that had run through an Upper East Side street, somewhere in the Nineties. The area had been evacuated with no loss of life, but the fire had caused widespread damage. There was a list of properties that had been gutted, and I was astonished to see a name I recognized. The Stevens Institute.

I'd finished for the day. Normally I'd have gone back to my hotel room to sleep before dinner, but on a whim I jumped on an uptown subway to take a look. With its still smoldering buildings, the burned-out street was closed off to the public, but from a corner vantage point I could make out where I thought the Stevens Institute had been. It was now an empty space between two facades that were blackened, but

structurally intact. I stood there a long moment staring into
the void, before turning away and making my way back to the
hotel. My mood on the journey back was subdued. Why had
I even gone up to the fire site? Perhaps I'd been seeking some
sort of relief, but instead I'd been left perplexed, anxious. I
took out my newspaper again and reread the article carefully,
with its list of destroyed buildings. None of the other names
meant anything to me.

Over the next few days I found myself brooding over the
fire. I was perturbed that I'd let it throw me like that, as lately
I'd managed to establish a certain balance in my life. I'd never
expected to last long as a stevedore, having had no previous
experience, but I'd slotted in and seemed to know instinctively what to do. The job itself was all consuming, physically
and mentally. No time to think during the long hours at the
docks; no energy to do so afterward. Life was reduced to a
simple routine of work, sleep, nourishment, and out of that
rigid pattern I could feel Smith emerging from me. On payday there'd be a night's carousing with fellow workers, since
Smith, unlike Manne, was a reasonably gregarious type. The
following morning I'd pay rent on my room, then eke out
whatever was left to me until the next pay. By the last day or
two, I'd often be broke. Sometimes I'd go without food, but I
didn't let it bother me much. I'd walk across downtown to my
hotel, giddy with hunger and fatigue, while at the same time
feeling a certain elation.

Before the fire, the idea of contacting my father had once
again been troubling me. I could save up the money somehow,
take a Greyhound bus down to Ohio and stay with him. He'd
written me, hadn't he? He'd extended a hand, which probably
meant he'd wanted one extended back. I thought of the one occasion when we'd met, me still a boy and him drunk. I imagined
how he must have regretted that down the years, how it would

have gnawed at him, how he would have wondered what had happened to me. And then, out of nowhere, someone from the hospital had contacted him. I was no longer a memory, a mental image. I was real, lying in a hospital bed. By now, he'd have cleaned up his act. No longer a drunkard, he'd remade his life and married again. He wanted to see his son and so he wrote him . . . For days I'd been absorbed in this little fantasy; the notion that I had a father out there who would welcome me into his family both comforted me and tore at me.

And then the fire. Something about it had intrigued; I'd bought a newspaper to find out more. There it was in black and white. The Stevens Institute had returned to my life at the very moment of its extinction—a harbinger of something I couldn't yet define. It meant, in any case, I hadn't yet escaped Manne. I tried to remember whether Dr. Peters had denied the existence of the Stevens Institute, and it seemed to me that he had. I still had my monthly appointment with him, and at the next one I could show him this newspaper. But why do that? Why destroy months of careful creation, both his and mine?

The more I mused on the story of the fire, the stranger it seemed. From my brief visit to the Stevens Institute, I'd received the impression of a moderately sized private hospital, with several wards and dozens of patients, some of them probably under heavy sedation. How could they have all been evacuated without loss of life, in the face of a fire fierce enough to have destroyed the entire building? You heard about properties gutted for insurance or other purposes. You saw it on the streets and read stories about it in the newspaper. Down at the docks, you heard gossip about mob-related arson. The Stevens Institute had been real enough, but what about its records, had they gone up in flames? Would there be any trace of Manne's visit there?

•

Payday had come around again. Life was like a concentrated seasonal cycle, wilting as the week progressed, then springing back each Friday afternoon, when we picked up our wages. Tonight, the drinking would be at Albert's Bar & Grill, a midtown den run by the friend of a fellow dockworker. We'd finished loading the *Marquise* for its five o'clock departure, and I'd gone straight to the accounts office to pick up my wages. I'd intended to go back to my room to change, which would have required a zigzag across town. In the end I found myself riding an uptown bus, getting off somewhere by Radio City. It wasn't often that I strayed into Manne's territory these days; there was something that made me feel inherently uneasy about it. Instinctively I pulled my hat low over my face as I walked down the street.

It was still early when I reached the bar. The few patrons there were mostly sitting by themselves, looking as if they hadn't moved in hours. Office workers were starting to trickle in, just ahead of rush hour, and the two worlds—that of the solitary drinkers and that of the workers—momentarily overlapped.

"What'll it be?"

"Give me a beer."

I downed the drink the bartender put before me and quickly ordered another. I gazed through the glass front into the streetscape, washed in the somber colors of the season. A smartly dressed man to my left stood stiffly by the bar, out of place as he stared into his beer glass. Despite his blank demeanor, I could tell from his eyes that he was in the grip of something, a huge emotion that he was barely containing. Perhaps he'd just been fired or something. His outward appearance vaguely reminded me of a colleague I'd once had, a man who'd killed himself following a personal tragedy. Our eyes engaged for a second or so before I looked away. Abruptly he drank up, paid up, then wandered out onto the street, standing outside the doors uncertainly for a good minute or so before moving out of view.

I was on my third or fourth beer, and half-drunk already when the other men from the docks arrived. I greeted those I knew, and the evening continued in a haze of noise and disorientation. Around me I could see people drinking, smoking, talking shop, talking women. After another hour or so it got rowdy. Someone mentioned politics before being roundly shouted down, albeit in a good-humored fashion. You could understand why. Politics, I now realized, was a passion for those with time to think. In the pared-down existence of the dockworker, what little free time and money you had was used to satiate far simpler pleasures.

I'd entered a fatigue-induced daydream. A face was there before me, the man who was buying me a drink. He was obviously one of the other stevedores, but I didn't particularly recognize him. It felt like we'd been talking for some time, but I could recall nothing of what had been said. As I drank the beer I felt I was watching the both of us from some neutral standpoint. At some point the man broke off from what he'd been saying and took a closer at me.

"But I know you, don't I? You're Smith."

I snapped out of my daydream.

"Yes. I'm Smith."

"We did a job together. Terminal up on Thirty-Fourth."

"I don't recall."

"You must. It was only a few years back. We used to go out drinking. We even came here once. You shared a room for a while with . . . who was it? Torma. Joe Torma. Remember him, don't you?"

"Yes. I remember Joe Torma."

"Poor old Joe. Ever hear what happened to him?

"No, I didn't."

"Drowned. Knocked off the quay by a swinging load."

"Good God."

"He was only thirty. We all pitched in to give him a good send-off. Company wouldn't lift a goddamn finger. You were long gone by then."

There was an uncomfortable pause while we both drained our glasses. For some reason I was thinking about the Stevens Institute. I couldn't get rid of this vision in my head of its smoldering, ghostly remains.

"Poor old Joe. But what about you? Where'd you go? Why'd you disappear like that?"

"The usual reasons. Trouble with the boss. Money trouble. Girl trouble."

"That reminds me. The woman you used to run around with. What was her name?"

"Marie."

"That's right. Marie. Spanish, isn't she?"

"French."

"I see her around sometimes. My wife knows her. She's a maid, I think. For a family somewhere around these parts. In one of those spanking new buildings. She used to talk about you. She used to ask after you."

"Did she? Do you know where I can find her?"

"I'll ask the missus. But where can she find you?"

"I'm at the Cravan Hotel, Third Avenue. If you see Marie, tell her she can leave a message for me there."

The evening was breaking up. A party of men had already left to blow the rest of their wages at a nearby brothel. One of the barmen was prodding a man asleep in his beer at the bar. Bottles and cigarette butts dotted the sawdust floor. Outside, the city cast an alien light over a homeless huddle sleeping under the awnings of a jeweler's store. Even here, the night had the power to transform everything into nebulous mystery. I made my way through the crowd of drunken revelers and found myself back at my hotel without knowing how I'd gotten there—as if I were already in a dream.

3

It was Saturday morning. I was supposed to be at work, but I'd called in sick. The foreman had been angry, and I'd lose the day's wages, but I didn't feel particularly concerned. I was horribly hungover, which put me in a heightened, nervy mood. I'd managed nonetheless to get downstairs while morning coffee was still being served. The breakfast room had a similar feel to the hospital's communal hall, and indeed a similar layout as well. Those who had work, or were trying to get some, had already left an hour earlier, but a few men remained slumped in the armchairs by the fire. They'd no doubt sit there all day, since it was fiercely cold outside. They'd sit there until they'd run out of money, and were kicked out of the hotel. That same fate could easily befall me if I lost my job.

As I drank the watery coffee, fragments of conversation from the night before came back to me. I recalled the man who'd claimed to have known Smith. Maybe there really was someone who'd worked on the docks a few years back and who'd borne some resemblance to me. But why had he told me that Joe Torma had been killed in an accident, when in fact I'd seen him a month or two before in the hospital? Perhaps he'd been mistaken, or I'd heard him wrong, or he'd been playing some kind of joke on me. It seemed that as Smith gradually solidified, the rest of the world reconfigured itself in order to account for his presence, albeit imperfectly. Just as, at the same time, it erased the traces of Manne from the city's streets.

Outside, snow swirled into never-settling patterns over the city. I climbed the Third Avenue El stairs opposite the hotel, and while waiting on the platform, I turned out my pockets and came up with a few dollars and some change. It was all I had to live on until next Friday—I'd gone through the rest the night before. A train clattered into the station. I took it up to Fifty-Ninth Street, then made my way back on foot to the corner of Fifty-Sixth and First. I was in front of my old apartment building again, now almost a picturesque ruin with the snow blowing into its broken windows. On the left inside the iron gates, the building's mailboxes were dilapidated. My eyes instinctively swiveled toward the lower right-hand corner, where Manne's box had been. It was still there, and Manne's name was still marked on it. Mail and advertising material were stuffed into its mouth. I cast around until I found an old trash can lid, which I used to knock off the lock. I flicked through the pile of bills, tax notices, and other official-looking letters. Only one card caught my attention. I recognized the handwriting:

You weren't at the funeral, why not? I need to speak to you. There is something I have to tell you. Please give me a call.

The card had been sent in early October; it was now late February. I folded it in half and put it in my pocket. An intense sadness invaded me, a pity for Manne, as though he were an entity outside me. He'd died like a dog. No one had thought to empty his mailbox, or even remove his name from it. Who would have settled his affairs? The city had closed in on his life, compressed it until there was nothing—only a few unpaid bills, a file in an administrative building. A name on a mailbox.

I made my way upstairs with trepidation. The building had never been particularly well maintained, but it was now scattered with garbage and debris, clearly unlived in. I stood outside my door. It had been forced, kicked in probably, and swung almost imperceptibly on its hinges as if it too were shivering with cold. The shadows I could see behind it unnerved me, and I didn't immediately go in. Instead I climbed halfway up the next flight of stairs. I knelt down and felt under the now tattered carpet and pulled out a key, my key. It was superfluous, of course. But in my hand it momentarily felt like an instrument of magic—a way back to Manne, should I ever want it. I pushed the door open. How many thousands of times had I done that, and seen this same view of my tiny hallway? The image was so deeply embedded that it wasn't just a memory, it was an integral part of me. Only now, for the first time, it was different. The wallpaper had been partially stripped, exposing the brickwork, and holes had been knocked into the wall. I tried the light switch but it didn't work; looking up toward the ceiling I could see wires gouged out and hanging down. I stood there and stared at the walls for some time—partly because of their unsettling effect on me, partly out of a fear of penetrating farther. The hanging wires and peeling wallpaper revealed my apartment's superficial claim to existence, its essential artifice. And yet it had not entirely disappeared, nor had its replacement entirely manifested itself. I was in a transitional space, awaiting its metamorphosis.

Now I walked through to what had been the front room—hesitantly, because I couldn't rid myself of the irrational expectation that I might see Manne in there, or his ghost at least. The room had been largely gutted, its furnishings removed. The only objects I recognized were the table and two chairs, pushed to a corner and covered in plaster dust. I briefly imagined workers clearing out the place, but leaving the table and chairs until last so they could have something to put their tools on, eat their lunch off. I picked up what I'd thought was a half-dollar from the table, but rubbing the dust off I was disappointed to see that it was a foreign denomination. I felt a tremendous urge to smoke, and went through the various pockets of my threadbare coat, but was completely out of cigarettes.

The bedroom. Despite its transformation—an entire inner wall had been knocked down—I could still see in my mind's eye how I'd left it for the last time: the bed, with Smith's comatose body upon it, and Abby's painting hanging behind. The nude in that painting had been staring into a room that wasn't there—only now it *was* miraculously there. The removal of the wall had in fact left an opening to another room: the builders were obviously joining two apartments together to create a grander, more upmarket residence. I'd often fantasized about what the other apartment on my floor would look like inside, and now I could see. For years it had been occupied by an unmarried woman, neither plain nor beautiful, who had seemed to lead as routine an existence as myself, leaving for work and returning home at exactly the same hours each day. Occasionally I'd hear the muffled sounds of a radio program from her apartment, just as she probably heard gramophone records from mine. But apart from that, there was only one time I'd ever been disturbed by her. After I'd gone to bed one night I'd heard voices through the wall—a man and a woman. That had surprised me, because I'd never noticed her having visitors before. At first the tone of the conversation had been neutral, but later it had become more heated, and finally there was shouting. Not long after, a door had slammed and I'd gathered that the man had left. For the next hour or so I'd heard soft sobbing, then finally nothing. I'd stayed awake for hours afterward, though, unable to sleep. The morning after, I'd seen her on the stairs, and wondered whether she might apologize for the noise of the night before. But she'd simply given me the same curt nod we'd always exchanged by way of acknowledging each other's presence. Nonetheless, I'd thought I'd detected a minute change to her face. A week or so later, it had occurred to me that I hadn't seen or heard her for several days. It took another week for it to hit home that she was no longer there. She'd been in her early thirties when she'd moved in, her late thirties when she'd moved out.

Something stopped me from actually stepping over the rubble into the other apartment, but from where I was standing I could see that it was the mirror image of my own. There were marks on the floor made by the legs of her bed: we'd been sleeping inches apart, separated only by the wall. The faded wallpaper was the same, as was the view through the window onto the courtyard. How many times had she and I unknowingly gazed out at the same time to the brick wall opposite? In the years we'd lived on the same floor, we'd barely addressed a word to each other. And yet there was that peculiar intimacy of living so close to someone, of seeing them every day.

To save money I walked back to the hotel—a long ramble

down an icy Third Avenue, stopping off on the way at a soup kitchen at St. Marks, where I queued up for something to eat. I passed a phone booth, and suppressed an urge to call Jeff Speelman. I'd even checked the number on the card he'd sent me, before stopping myself. Why was I still chasing Manne? Why couldn't I let him alone, when I had this new life before me? I wondered what Speelman had wanted to see Manne about. Perhaps Abby had left me something in her will. Perhaps Speelman wanted to give me back some of the things that Abby had taken on our separation. Or was it the reverse? Did he want Abby's painting, the one that had hung over our bed? I stood there in the street, staring at the people scurrying in and out of the cold. I could feel myself on the brink of tears. The old apartment key was in my pocket, and an uncanny sensation lingered within me.

There'd been a message slip for me at the front desk of the hotel. I'd assumed it was someone from the shipping company, and didn't bother to unfold it until I was upstairs in my room. It read: "Marie Wilders. 12:45 p.m. No.: GR 5-9975." That was all. I poked about in my coat pocket for a nickel and went to the phone in the hallway. The operator let it ring on the other end for a long time before she finally cut in: "No answer." Back in my room I tossed the slip onto my bedside table, beside Speelman's card. The light was fading; I hadn't realized it was that late. It was one of those days you float through without ever really knowing the time.

I lay down on my bed and let my mind drift back, just as I'd used to do in the hospital. I was thinking about Miss Fregoli again. About how her mother had written me, a year or so after her daughter's suicide. Somehow she'd come across the article I'd published about the case, and had guessed the identity of the patient even though I'd used a pseudonym for her. She'd enclosed Miss Fregoli's two-page suicide note. "I don't want it, I never want to see it again, but perhaps it might be of use to you in your studies," she'd written. The note itself was something else: an abstract, measured, elegantly written disquisition on life and death. It had confounded me, not only because it didn't sound like anything Miss Fregoli could have written, but also because it was unlike any other suicide note I'd seen in my time as a psychiatrist. They were rarely contemplative or metaphysical. On the contrary, they tended to be short, flat, even practical—one that had always stuck in my mind had simply said: "Don't forget to feed the cat." And then a couple of years after receiving that letter from Miss Fregoli's mother, sitting in a restaurant in Central Park on a warm spring day, I'd been reading a Balzac novel. In it, a young woman kills herself and leaves a letter, quoted in the novel. I'd been astonished to discover that parts of it were word for word the same as Miss Fregoli's. She'd told me in one of our last appointments that she'd been reading Balzac. That must have been in the back of my mind while I'd been browsing the shelves of the Gotham Book Mart for something to read. I'd spent the rest of that day wandering around the Park, wrestling with the implications of my discovery. Miss Fregoli's note—which had on some level moved me, even seduced me—hadn't meant what it had literally said. It now seemed to me like an airless, mirthless joke. I'd understood nothing of her, I'd realized.

I shook my head. Why couldn't I leave the memories alone? Manne was the dive inward, when what I needed was the opposite. I got up, fished out my nickel again, went back to the phone. Once more, the ringing went on and on until the operator broke in: "No one answering."

"Let it ring another minute."

"Ain't no one answering."

"Let it ring."

"Suit yourself, mister."

The wind rattled the windows behind me, the vibrations resolving to a single, plaintive note. I'd been seized with this idea that contacting Marie would render Smith more concrete, deepen his character, and give him more of a life. Wouldn't it in fact have the reverse effect? What would happen when she realized that I wasn't whoever she thought I was? I managed to put that thought aside. I recalled the woman I used to see on the balcony, back at the hospital, and the way she'd stared back at me. That simple, repeated encounter had been perfect in its way, perfectly unreal as well.

I still had the receiver to my ear, and the ringing cut out abruptly—for a second I thought the operator had terminated the call. Then I heard a click and a tentative "Yes?" It was a female voice, one that I couldn't place, but that nonetheless reminded me of someone, somewhere.

4

"Do you remember that place where we used to meet?"

"Which place?"

"The French café. Do you remember?"

"I'm not sure."

"We used to go there for a drink, before a movie. It had a long, polished bar."

"I remember it now. Le Zinc."

"It's not there any more. I walked down that street the other day. It's around the corner from where I work. The café's gone."

"What's there now?"

"Just a bar and grill. They changed the decor. It doesn't look anything like the old place. It was strange going in."

Marie was silent for a moment. She reached out, gently put her hand to my cheek. I flinched; her touch had sent a tiny shock through my body. It was the first physical contact I'd had with a woman in a while.

"How did that happen?"

"Accident. I fell onto the rails at a subway station."

"It's changed you."

"It's disfigured me."

"You don't have the same face. You're different, that's all."

Her hand was still on my cheek: I put my own over hers. My scar, which had never healed properly, didn't seem to displease her. Before, I'd been ashamed of it, but on hearing her words, I understood that it could be seen from another perspective. Perhaps it could even be appealing, under a certain light. After all, there were women who liked imperfection in a man.

"I haven't asked why you left."

"I don't know how I could explain it."

"It doesn't matter now. I guess you called at the right time. If I'd heard from you even a week earlier, I might have put the phone down."

I grabbed the waiter as he passed, ordered more drinks, and pulled out the wallet I'd pickpocketed from a dozing drunk on the subway ride up—it was full of bills, two weeks' wages worth at least. All the time we'd been sitting in the booth by the window, Marie had been staring at me, and I'd turned away, hiding behind my hands, behind my drink. I'd been looking through the glass front of the bar, and had allowed myself to become fixated on a man loitering on the other side of the road; I'd entertained the absurd fantasy that he was spying on me. But my intuition that Marie wasn't repelled by my disfigurement freed me up. Now I felt I could bear the ferocity of her gaze. I, in turn, examined her properly for the first time. Dark hair, olive skin, trim figure. Her face was careworn and she was probably younger than she looked. I had the impression that she'd undergone a major trial, and despite pulling through, had remained diminished by it.

We'd both been acting stiffly and awkwardly, me even more markedly than her. But by the second drink we'd eased up, leaning into each other over the table. The past, real or imagined, was the silent backdrop to a conversation that in itself remained determinedly in the present. I listened to Marie as she talked about her work as a maid, at the midtown apartment of a divorcé and his young son; I told her something of the life down by the docks. The talk was muted, effortless. All too quickly it was time to go. Marie glanced at her watch: "I've got to see someone. I told you I only had an hour."

I helped her out of the booth. Outside the bar, we stood on the sidewalk looking at each other. The strain of melancholy, admittedly there from the moment I'd heard her voice on the phone, was now all too palpable.

"The French café. The last time we met there, the very last. We talked about living together. Do you remember?"

"I remember."

"And then you left."

"I'll make it up to you. If you want me to."

By way of answering, she kissed me briefly on the cheek. There was a pause, as if we both knew it wasn't enough. I embraced her, and at the same time felt her hands pressing into me. We must have been in each other's arms for a minute or so before she eventually disentangled herself.

"I'll always want the best for you."

"I know."

She strode off without looking back. I stood there on the sidewalk for quite some time, staring at the corner around which she'd disappeared. Eventually I wandered back into the subway. I put my hand to my cheek: it felt wet. I wasn't sure whether they were my tears, or hers, from when she'd put her face to mine.

On the ride home, I felt in a daze. I'd thought of walking

back to the hotel, despite the cold, but the bar Marie had asked
me to meet her at was somewhere way up on the Upper West
Side, and it was too far. The melancholy lingered the length
of the subway trip. It was coupled with an uneasy, exhilarat-
ing sensation of once more being thrown into the middle of
a story I'd only half-understood. I couldn't work out what
might have gone through Marie's mind when she'd first caught
sight of me. She'd seemed to recognize me. Perhaps, with the
distancing effect of my facial injuries, she'd convinced herself
that I really was whoever she'd mistaken me for. In my gut I
knew that wasn't the case. It was more complicated than that.
Stories I'd made up in the hospital about Smith had seemingly taken on a life of their own. Why shouldn't they have?
After all, I'd simply put together the hard-luck clichés of any
number of my patients. That they should be collectively true,
for someone, somewhere in New York, didn't strike me as unlikely. It was an illusion, this feeling that Smith was warping
the surrounds.

Not quite ready to go back to the hotel after all, I got off
the subway at a random station and found myself somewhere in the theater district. It was a glacial Saturday night.
The crowds were out, milling about in their various tribes.
The dinner-and-show people, the out-of-towners, the sailors
on leave, the neatly dressed guys outside hotels waiting for
their dates. Intensely familiar scenes, ones I felt disconnected
from. I stopped outside a bar for a few minutes. In a booth
on the other side of the glass I spied a love-struck couple in
earnest conversation. It had always beguiled me, when you
could see people converse but not hear them, like in a silent
movie. I watched them for quite a while until the man looked
up at me, questioningly. I walked on, down Forty-Second. I
thought of Marie touching my face, and put my hand to my
scar. "Hows about it mister," murmured a thin girl from the

side exit of one of the theaters. A low light cast her infinite shadow down the street.

A block on, and I was outside the Century. The last time I'd been there, Abby had been smiling at me from a poster of a show she'd been in with the Lunts. Now there was another show on, still with the Lunts. Perhaps it was even the same play, but with a different sidekick. Abby, too, had been excised, erased. Finally, I realized, she was gone. So absent that it was almost as though she'd never been there. Now there was Marie. I knew that I wanted to go to bed with her. I looked down at my feet. A little plaque had been embedded in the sidewalk, a memorial to those who'd lost their lives in a theater fire.

Marie. Somehow you could tell that as a young girl she'd been plain and gawky, although she wasn't now. She must have grown into her face, the way men often did, but which was rarer for a woman. What mattered to me right now was that for Marie, our encounter in the bar had probably signaled the end of something—the final scene. Whereas I was determined for it to be a beginning.

5

"Why did you want to get off here?"

"Can't you guess?"

Marie and I were climbing out of the subway on East Broadway. It was the next day, Sunday. Streets that would normally be bustling and animated—filled with stalls and street peddlers—were now deserted, sinister. We made our way through the grids of tenement blocks, down to Manhattan Bridge, then walked for a half hour or so along the river, past the old oyster houses and piers—most of them in a state of decrepitude since the switch of shipping traffic to the other side of the island.

"There. You came out from there."

Marie was pointing to a door that hung limply from its hinges. After the wordless wandering, we'd stopped by an old warehouse fronted by an abandoned office, and a peeling sign that said COIMBRA SHIPPING. I pushed through the door, unsure of what I was supposed to find. Inside, a mess of broken furniture, beer bottles, piles of paper and garbage, floorboards pulled up to reveal mud and dirt. The vestiges of an office, now crumbled away into a nighttime refuge for the homeless. A calendar was still pinned to the wall, marked with faded, handwritten scribbles and annotations. Mold had eaten half of it away but there was enough detail to tell that it only dated from the year before. It surprised me that this could have been a working office as recently as that. The space was dead. It smelled musky, as if its abandonment had happened decades and not months ago.

I went back outside. For a second I couldn't see Marie but then I spotted her on the sidewalk, sitting on a tattered case that she must have pulled from a nearby pile of refuse.

"Do you remember?"

I had the feeling of our relationship mysteriously coming back to me, piece by piece. It wasn't the first time I'd caught myself thinking of her as someone I'd been with, and had inexplicably let go. As I watched her sitting on the case I couldn't help imagining her naked on a bed, propped up on an elbow, looking up to me. It was like a memory.

"Come on, let's grab some coffee."

She nodded. We turned from the river and walked down streets I didn't know, our hands interlaced although I had no sense of how or when they'd become so. We found a coffee place on a street corner in an Italian enclave and sat looking at each other intently over the cups. A welter of thoughts came to me but I was waiting for Marie to say something first. I realized that we'd hardly spoken since we'd agreed to meet that morning.

"You've changed . . . I've changed too."

"You seem the same to me."

She shook her head: "When I met you, I could hardly speak English."

"It didn't matter, though, did it? We went to a movie together that first time. You seemed to enjoy it."

"I couldn't understand it. I remember you miming the
story to me afterward. I'd dreamed up a completely different
version in my mind."

"Now your English is so good—how did it get that way?"

"There was an old woman at the refugee bureau. She gave
classes for free. She took an interest in me. I was seeing her
every day. I decided I had to learn properly, if I wanted to
make a life here."

"And you did learn. So why are you still working as a
maid?"

"It's not hard. It doesn't take up much time. I owe it to the
man I'm working for. He took me in. After you'd left me with
nothing."

I was silent for a moment.

"The man. Tell me about him."

"He's kind. He's alone. Divorced. His ex-wife lives in
Brooklyn. She has medical problems. Sometimes his young
son is there with him, sometimes not. Sometimes he travels,
and then there's no one in the apartment."

"You stay there?"

"Yes."

"What's his name?"

"Mr. Stevenson."

"Are you sleeping with him?"

"No. I share a room with the little boy."

"What do you do when they're not there?"

"I have the place to myself. I get up, do a little housework.
Hang the clothes on the line. Smoke a cigarette on the balcony. I get dressed. I study."

"What are you studying?"

"Don't you remember?"

"No."

"I will take the medical exams, when I'm ready."

"How can you afford to do this? Is Stevenson paying for you?"

"Yes. He's paying for me."

"Don't you think he'll want something in return, eventually?"

"He's already getting something in return. I'm looking after his son. I'm looking after his apartment."

"Is he there now?"

"No."

"What about his son?"

"He's upstate, with his grandparents."

"Why don't we go to the apartment, now?"

"All right. If you want."

"You're sure?"

"I'm sure."

Not a word was spoken in the cab. But where the silence of the river walk had been easy, it had now become taut with expectation. As if our final exchange in the coffee bar had constituted a binding contract, and there was nothing further to be done. My mind was jolting forward, replaying scenes to come as if they'd already happened. We passed through streets I thought I knew, but when I looked out the window to identify something specific—a store, a building, a landmark—I couldn't come up with anything. We weren't holding hands now; Marie's rested on her lap. A thick woolen scarf obscured her neck and the lower half of her face.

"This is the place."

The cab halted outside a new, well-heeled block that I recognized from some former incarnation. I paid off the driver, and a liveried doorman stepped out onto the sidewalk to open the door for Marie. She nodded briefly and we entered the lobby, whose plastic opulence recalled to mind my old office building on Park Avenue. We rode up to a middling floor. Once we'd gotten out, and the operator had pulled the elevator doors shut, Marie fiddled about under the carpet for the key.

We were inside. With a single, sweeping glance, I felt I'd understood all I needed to know. Neat, functional, the apartment was smaller than I'd thought it would be. It was the home of a tidy, methodical man, in no great need of a maid. I had the image of an ordinary-looking, middle-aged professional, whose uneventful life had been broken open by the unexpected departure of his wife. In the wake of that catastrophe, he had no doubt turned inward. When not caring for his child, I imagined, his life would have become consumed in a series of increasingly private routines and rituals. Things might have gone on terminally like this, but for a singular encounter. Perhaps he'd been eating at his usual place, the one he went to every day without fail, and then he'd spotted a striking, forlorn young woman, sitting on a suitcase across the street. Perhaps it had started like that.

All of this had come to me in a second. Impossible to imagine a man and a woman living here, in this smallish space, without sleeping together, it occurred to me. You could feel it in the walls. But I didn't find the thought particularly troubling. Marie had gotten out of her coat; she'd thrown it over a chair and now turned to me.

"Do you remember this dress?"

Simple, patterned, demure, it was nothing out of the ordinary, and it took me a moment to work out why the dress looked strange. It was a cotton summer outfit, and we were in the depths of winter.

"I remember."

The heavy coat had betrayed nothing of her body. She

slipped the straps from her shoulders and put her arms around my neck. I kissed her and she pulled away, kicking off her shoes and shimmying free of her dress. As she undid her bra I glanced toward the balcony with its French windows that were slightly ajar, despite the cold. When I looked back, Marie was in her stockings, otherwise naked. She stood framed by an inner doorway, its straight lines accentuating the contours of her breasts and hips. It was how I'd imagined her; the erotic pull felt familiar.

She was gazing through to another room that I couldn't see at first. I thought she was looking at someone, even signaling to him, but when I walked over to her, there was no one. Only an empty space, save for two narrow beds. We hurriedly pushed them together. Marie reached down to unbutton my pants. She whispered something, too softly for me to catch it. My hand was on her breast, her hand on mine, my head full of the smell of her skin. Inside the moment she seemed barely recognizable, her flesh almost liquid to touch. But behind the distorting excitement I was aware of something else, an almost comfortable intimacy. As if this were something we'd done a hundred times before.

"When's he back?"

"This afternoon."

"I'd better leave, then."

"Don't go just yet. He'll call first."

Marie had propped herself on her elbow. She was looking up at me, and her face had a radiance that startled me. I put my hand to her neck, and traced the faint white line that ran from below her ear down to her shoulder blade.

"What's this?"

"From an operation."

"What for?"

"I had a tumor. Years ago. But you knew that."

She turned about so I could no longer see the scar. Perhaps the fact of having one herself had softened her toward my own. She'd worn her scarf high up on her neck, just as I tended to push my fedora down over my face.

It felt like the greatest luxury to watch Marie as she dressed without hurry. She disappeared into the bathroom. I put the beds back to how they'd been, then wandered out into the small corridor, at the end of which was another bedroom, its door half open. The man's room. Perhaps Marie's as well. Without thinking, I walked in. Double bed, a chest of drawers, a small writing table, a wardrobe—just by looking around I felt I already knew him. What kind of man would call his maid to say he was on his way home, I wondered. No kind of man, evidently. I opened the wardrobe: a dozen or so white shirts hung neatly off a railing, seemingly all the same. Had Marie ironed them? I took one off the hanger and put it on; it fit me perfectly. I'd torn my own shirt in my haste to get undressed. Some ten-dollar bills, maybe a dozen of them, sat on the bedside table. For what purpose? I picked up a couple but then put them down again. I didn't want to get Marie into trouble.

I turned around to see her watching me from the sitting room. She was no longer wearing the summer dress, but a more seasonal woolen skirt and cardigan. Her hair was smoothed down, makeup applied. She was different again, her face more serious, and in her difference, our sexual encounter of only minutes before seemed inconceivable. As if to reassure myself that it had happened, I walked up to her and put my hands around her waist. I started to unbutton her cardigan.

"There's no time."

"Will we see each other again?"

"I don't know."

"If you don't know, why did you go to bed with me?"

She turned away and sat down in the one armchair in the room. Beside it was a small table on which lay some medical books.

"You disappear completely. Suddenly you're back again. I'm angry with you. Very angry. But not quite finished with you. Remember the time we met outside Radio City?

"Yes."

"You knew a way to get into the show without paying. We couldn't afford to eat out, but you had flowers for me. Later you told me you'd spent an hour picking them in Central Park."

"I remember."

She nodded to herself. It all made strange sense to me. Manne had been cold, austere, driven by routine; Smith was different: gregarious, impulsive—even romantic, it seemed. As Marie excavated the details of our affair, it came alive for me as well, the scenes playing in my head like a movie reel. I tried to imagine what it must have been like for her, a refugee, arriving in New York, knowing no one, utterly alone. But then someone eventually takes pity on you. He makes an effort to help you. It almost doesn't matter who he is, or that he barely shares a common language with you. In fact, the greater the distance between the two of you, the better it is. After all, passion is not a meeting of minds, it's an entanglement of fantasies. Only later, as the unknown is gradually, dismally translated into the known, does the disappointment come.

The ringing phone cut through my thoughts. Marie hurried over to the sideboard and picked it up.

"Yes ... yes ... Anatole ... yes." She put down the receiver and turned to me. "You've got to go now."

"That was Stevenson?"

"Yes. He's at Grand Central."

"Anatole . . . you're on first name terms with him?"

"That's his son's name."

"He has a French name?"

"No. It's just my own name for him. A kind of joke."

"What sort of joke?"

"A silly thing. It's not important."

She put her arms around my neck again, and I could feel her breasts against me. She had a pet name for the boy, one that she shared with his father. Even in the unlikely event that she wasn't sleeping with Stevenson, it demonstrated a certain domestic intimacy. I had an image of her here in the apartment playing with the boy, the man looking on indulgently, like an illustration for an ad.

"Will we see each other again?"

"Don't worry. We'll see each other again."

6

It took me quite a while to find the hospital again, despite the midtown location. When I finally came upon it, practically by accident, its modest facade seemed to slot perfectly into a faceless New York. Through the doors I found myself in an atrium, with a reception desk at one end manned by a young man, no doubt a medical student earning a few extra bucks. I remembered little of the day of my discharge, only a couple of months before, although it felt like the distant past. Now I took the opportunity to look about and absorb the details. Fresh paint, shiny carpet, new chairs—and yet, in my mind, the hospital had been quite shabby. It must have been renovated in the months since I'd left. Nobody about, which was odd as well. As if to contradict that thought, a woman suddenly appeared from behind the receptionist's desk and then walked out the front door. For a bizarre moment I thought she was Marie, although on second glance the resemblance was quite superficial.

I was in a waiting area just off the atrium. I'd had my

misgivings about coming back to the hospital for the appointment. I had this image of it as a sort of cocoon. A place of flickering ambiguity, into which a dying Manne had entered, and a reborn Smith had exited. It should have disappeared and crumbled away as soon as I no longer had any use for it. Now I wondered whether Dr. Peters might even get me committed again. I had a desire to melt back into the city, to become yet another of its anonymous faces. Instead, I'd kept my word. I didn't really know why, except that it was to do with Manne, not Smith. I couldn't entirely shake Manne off, not on my own.

"Dr. Peters will see you now."

A nurse had appeared. She led me down a long corridor to an elevator. As we walked, I continued to look around, surprised at how perfect everything seemed. Even the nurse herself was immaculately groomed, as if she'd just stepped out of a makeup department. We rode the elevator, walked down another pristine corridor, and then the nurse said: "This is Dr. Peters's office."

I'd had this notion that the meeting would be in the room I'd occupied at the hospital, just like old times. I'd even felt a vague longing to be back there. But the moment I actually thought about it, I realized the absurdity of the idea. Now I stood by a door that was half open. I could see the doctor not directly, but in a mirror on the wall facing his desk. Opposite, in a position I could see neither directly nor indirectly, was another man, whose voice I recognized. My first doctor at the hospital: the one with the beard, the pince-nez, the patrician New England accent. "I don't think it's the right way to go about things, not at all," I could hear him say, to which Dr. Peters replied, "I'm afraid it's no longer up to you." There was another testy exchange, then the squeak of a chair leg scraping across the linoleum. The man walked past me, without so much as casting a glance in my direction.

"Mr. Smith? Come in. Please, sit down."

Dr. Peters had been taking notes, and continued to do so for a minute or so, ignoring me as I sat there silently—it was a technique I remembered using myself, as a means of inducing unease and weakening a patient's resistance. Finally, he left off. He opened a dossier on his desk and glanced through it.

"So . . . a stevedore . . . Chelsea Piers . . . seems you've been absent from work quite a few days. Why is that?"

"I got sick. I'm back on the job now."

"Well . . . I wouldn't take any more time off if I were you."

Another minute's silence while Dr. Peters read through notes, ignoring me. I looked about the office, which seemed utterly ordinary. There was the desk photo of his wife, another of two young boys. Each perfectly posed, with just the right smiles. As if they were not real family portraits, but a studio demonstration of what a family portrait should look like.

"Tell me about Marie."

"What about her?"

"You've been seeing her again, haven't you?"

"That's right."

"Tell me about it."

"We got back in touch, through a mutual acquaintance. A few weeks back. That's all there is to it."

"What do you do together?"

"We go to the movies. The usual stuff."

"That's it? Nothing in particular she likes to do?"

"Like what?"

"Anything. Anything that comes to mind."

"Well . . . she likes to go back to places we've been to before."

"How do you mean?"

"We went down to the Battery, for example. She told me about the time we went there when we were first seeing each other. She wanted to retrace our steps."

"What do you make of that?"

"I don't make anything of that."

"I see. Where do you usually meet?"

"In coffee shops, bars. One in particular I guess. Albert's Bar & Grill. I kind of know the guy who runs it."

"What I meant was, where do you conduct your affair? At your hotel?"

"No. We tried that once. We were caught out. In fact, the manager's given me notice."

"What will you do?"

"I don't know."

"Well, where have you and Marie been sleeping together?"

"She works for a family, not far from here. She has the run of the apartment when they're not there, which is a lot of the time."

"You sleep in the marital bed?"

"No. We sleep in a different room."

"Have you made any plans together?"

"You mean like getting married?"

"Any sort of plans."

"Not really . . . Marie talks about a place upstate. The people she works for have a vacation home up that way. On a lake. She says we should borrow the house in the spring. Get away from the city."

"What do you think of that idea?"

"I don't know."

"How would you like a place of your own? Here in the city?"

"I'd like it pretty well. But there's not much chance of that."

The doctor opened a desk drawer and took out a typed

sheet, read it through, signed it at the bottom, and sealed it into an envelope. He picked up the phone, dialed a number, murmured a few yeses and nos into the receiver. He turned to me: "Can you afford thirty dollars a month?"

"I think so."

A few more murmurs and then he put down the receiver. He scribbled something on a piece of paper and handed it to me.

"This is the address of a rental agent. Here's a letter for him. Go see him now. He's waiting for you."

The interview was over; it had lasted barely ten minutes. I was escorted back down the corridors and walked quickly out through the lobby. It was a surprise to so suddenly find myself on the sidewalk again, and it took me a moment to gather my thoughts. Crossing the street, I turned around briefly to look back at the hospital facade, but it had already been swallowed up into the streetscape.

The address the doctor had scrawled was on the Lower East Side. I'd have to get the F train down to East Broadway, again. I went through the motions—climbing down the stairs, putting the nickel in the turnstile, finding my way onto the platform—but my mind was still occupied with Dr. Peters. There were things I'd wanted to ask him, but I'd been fazed by the meeting's abrupt end. I could understand how he'd known about my absenteeism. Someone at the shipping company must be reportig back to the hospital. But Marie? How could he have known that I was seeing her? It threw up the possibility of something far more insidious. I eyed the two men opposite me on the train. One was wearing a suit and reading the *Times*; the other was more raggedly dressed, probably a vagrant. Neither was paying any attention to me; neither were likely candidates to be spies.

In my hands was Dr. Peters's letter, sealed in an envelope,

and I resisted the urge to tear it open. It was no doubt some sort of institutional guarantee on the rental of an apartment. Why should he offer me that? I had the impression of being toyed with. I was a laboratory rat that Dr. Peters had set free in the city, to see how I'd react. A paranoid reaction on my part, but then the interview had felt almost designed to induce paranoia. I remembered my own time as a psychiatrist, and how a patient's paranoia would inevitably become fixated on the treatment itself, provoking the very symptoms it was designed to banish. Of course, I could easily get off the train now and throw away the address the doctor had given me. I could easily disappear into the city. But I was being offered a place to live just as I was about to lose my hotel room, during a bitter winter.

Now I was at the agent's office, above a grocery store. The agent read the doctor's letter carefully with what seemed to me some puzzlement. He spoke to someone on the phone, possibly Dr. Peters, then finally opened a cupboard and took out some keys. I followed him from the office, down to a dingy street of tenement buildings, fifteen minutes' walk away. We made our way up the garbage-strewn stairway of a rundown building, to a door on the third floor. Beyond it, a smallish room with peeling walls, a table and two chairs, a sofa, a bad painting hanging opposite a tiny window. An opening in the far wall led to an identically sized room, with just a mattress on the floor. The agent sat down on one of the chairs and lit a cigarette without offering me one. He was a stocky, square-jawed man and he wore a plain dark suit.

"You want it?"

"I'll take it."

"Okay. You're set 'til the end of the month. After that you gotta pay upfront."

"All right."

He put the key on the table.

"You come down and see me at the end of the month, okay?"

"Okay."

I was alone again. I looked around the apartment. It wasn't so different in its basic structure from the one I'd inhabited for so many years, farther uptown. It would need some fixing up to be presentable enough for Marie—a coat of paint at the very least. Nonetheless, I felt a surge of exhilaration. I opened the door that the agent had just closed, and looked out onto the drab landing with its stained carpet. Somebody was scraping about in the apartment opposite. I crossed the landing and knocked, thinking I might introduce myself as the new tenant—there were one or two questions I could ask about the building as well. I could hear labored breathing from the other side of the door. I knocked again, but no one answered.

No bathroom was inside the apartment; it was probably in the hall. But a small sink nestled in the corner. I threw my head under some running water, then smoothed back my wet hair and looked into the mirror fixed to the wall. It was dirty and warped, and a distorted version of myself stared back. In some fundamental way, though, I hadn't changed as much as I'd supposed. Beyond the scar, beyond the more recent signs of ageing and my now-graying hair, it was the same mask as always. You tilt your head and things look different—what had become unfamiliar is familiar once more. You realize that it's the same face. That it's been there all this time, no matter how far you stray, waiting patiently for you, there in the looking glass.

7

Marie was getting dressed. I was lying on the mattress, watching her. It was fiercely cold, and I wasn't expecting to go out much today. I hadn't officially quit my job, but I'd had a run-in with the foreman, and I wasn't necessarily going to return. No matter. Work seemed relatively easy to come by at the moment, and the other day I'd had some luck in the subway as well, pickpocketing a fat businessman's wallet stuffed with bills.

"Where are you going?"

"College."

A professor at Columbia was helping Marie with her studies. It was someone I vaguely remembered from my own time there. People she was meeting knew Manne, and although the name was unlikely ever to come up in conversation, the connection still felt strange. Marie was now bent over, applying lipstick in the small, cracked mirror.

"You're not going to the other apartment?"

"No."

"You're not looking after Anatole today?"

"No."

I knew she didn't like me using the name Anatole—the boy's real name was Anthony. It was like an accusation, intruding on her intimacy with the boy and his father. I was silent as she put the finishing touches to her makeup. A few minutes later she was gone, the click of the door echoing in the emptiness. The apartment was peculiarly silent for its downtown location, and those first few moments of solitude were always slightly eerie. I hadn't made the place a home, as I'd planned to. It hadn't come alive. The walls were still bare, excepting the mirror and the clumsy painting of a seaside scene. I'd cleaned the place up, I'd painted the walls, I'd bought curtains and sheets. But that was as far as it had gone.

At first I'd insisted Marie move in with me. She'd stayed a week or so—even then I'd noticed that she hadn't brought all her things with her—but it wasn't long before she was back spending half of her nights with her employer. I could see well enough that the two apartments were escapes from each other, and I didn't say anything. Sometimes I felt in love with Marie; other times, there was a cold distance. I was beginning to understand Smith's vanishing act, although nothing like that would be necessary this time around. I could already see how things would pan out. A traumatized refugee had fallen for me, but now she was remaking herself. One day, she'd wear a white coat. She'd be a doctor with a foreign accent. Perhaps she'd land an internship at Bellevue, as I had. In years to come, she might even end up with an office on Park Avenue. Long before that, our worlds would have separated. She'd drop by less and less frequently. We'd have less to say to each other. The sex would become perfunctory, even clinical. Then one day, she simply wouldn't show up when she'd said she would, and that would be that. Just visualizing the sequence of events in my head seemed to make it a done deal. And as much as Marie had been important to me, I wouldn't have much trouble finding another woman. I'd had offers enough, in the bars I'd frequented.

I heard a door opening and closing across the landing. I jumped up to open my own door, but not fast enough. I'd only caught glimpses of the person who lived opposite me, and all I could say with any confidence was that she was a woman, either middle aged or old. She never answered when I knocked, and her shadowy presence played into my paranoia. In my weaker moments, even Marie could provoke suspicion. She was studying medicine. Did she have some connection with Dr. Peters? Other things about her didn't feel quite right. How had she learned to speak English so well, so quickly?

I thought I'd go out, after all. There was nothing to eat or drink in the apartment, and in any case a whole day inside would only result in cabin fever. I dressed and went down the stairs into a blast of freezing air, hugging myself tight. The extreme cold made you withdraw ever deeper into your core—just as the heat did the opposite, a relentless sun exploding one's sense of self. I went into an Italian place and ordered some coffee. Lying on the counter was a photo magazine, *Look* or something like that. I idly flicked my way through it, wondering what I might do for the rest of the day. I'd take a subway uptown. It was the kind of weather where I could spend the entire day in a theater, watching movie after movie until they spilled over into each other and then into my dreams.

The magazine pictures paraded past me in a blur of smiling faces. I froze, then turned back a few pages to a full-page ad. The bland, good-looking features of the woman in it were hard to place, and it took me a few seconds to work out who she was. Mrs. Esterhazy. I recalled thinking, the one time we'd met, that there was something flat and generic about her, as if she'd walked out of an ad for washing powder. And now here she was. Neither young nor old, part of an all-American scene, a husband returning from work and the young son playing with his train set on the living room floor. It didn't really matter what the advertisement was for. I slipped the magazine into my coat pocket and drank up my coffee.

A frozen mist hung over the city. It was late morning, but the light barely penetrated down to street level. Despite this gauziness, on Park Avenue South I felt I was suddenly able to see for miles and miles, intersection after intersection, past my old office, to Harlem River and beyond. Perhaps there was some sort of corridor through the fog at that precise point, or more probably it was my imagination. New York seemed like a vast machine. A city-sized puppet show, the wires almost visible, flickering in the periphery of my vision. People streamed down the avenue into the subway, as if part of a mass ritual. It was hard to get a sense of anyone as an individual, within that indiscriminate multitude. I focused on a woman with a small child, pregnant with another. I marveled at the optimism of giving birth to something that you knew would die one day. I pondered the significance of Mrs. Esterhazy's photo. Somehow, it meant that Manne was still there, in the shadows. And his story was still alive, despite my best efforts.

I climbed the stoop of my building, skipping the broken stair that had tripped me up the day before. I was back in my apartment now, and everything was exactly how I'd left it, naturally, even though it felt changed by what I'd found. The stillness and silence didn't induce calm, but a sort of anxiety of anticipation, a feeling that something would happen, must happen. I tore the photo out of the magazine and pinned it to the wall, then lay back down on the mattress, hands behind my head, examining it at leisure. On the one hand, it was

a rigorously conventional piece of advertising, no different
from hundreds of pictures you could find in any number of
publications. On the other hand, the more I looked at it, the
more the image seemed a world unto itself.

The setting was a split-level sitting room, traditional and
yet modern, probably in one of New York's tonier suburbs,
although the garish colors of the decor suggested California
as well—I had half of a feeling that I'd seen this same room in
other ads. A man has just come through the door, he's waving
to his wife and kid. His brown check suit and trilby aren't so-
ber enough for him to be a lawyer or a banker, but he's clearly
on a decent salary. Perhaps he's an ad man—after all, directors
make movies about Hollywood, novelists have novel-writing
protagonists, and maybe ad men create ads about ad men.
Each of the protagonists—the man, the woman, the child—is
caught in a pose of absolute expression, like in a nineteenth-
century academic painting. There's unalloyed joy in the man's
face as he greets his family: it's as if he's been away weeks,
rather than hours. But his expression seems forced, off-key.
Which is not exactly surprising, given that this is an advertisement, not a stolen photo of an actual homecoming. The
man in the picture is not a doting husband and father, after
all. He is a model, a bad actor.

And yet I couldn't entirely see it that way. I couldn't un-
suspend my disbelief so easily. I had to create a narrative that
accounted for all the details. For me, the man's strange grin
masked unease. It wasn't hard to think up a conventional explanation: for example, he might have stopped off at his mistress's apartment on the way home. But I had feeling that this
unease was something altogether more fundamental. Perhaps
the man has come back to his house, and as he opens the
door, ready to greet his wife and son, he sees a woman and
child he doesn't recognize. The boy jumps up to give him a

hug; the woman kisses him, then whispers an endearment in his ear. In shock, he lets all this happen, passively. He plays the part that is patently expected of him. There's a moment when he knows that he should confront the two, ask them who the hell they are, but that moment passes, and the man feels himself drawn into a story not his own. Perhaps some kind of joke is being played on him; perhaps he's the victim of a malaise; perhaps there are other forces at work. In any case, playing the game seems to be the path of least resistance, until he understands what's happening to him.

My gaze shifted from the man, to the furniture, to the boy, to his toy train in violent blue. Each detail of the scene would either be smoothly integrated into the narrative I'd created, or would shape it further. The one thing in the photograph that I seemed to be avoiding was Mrs. Esterhazy herself. Her face bore a similar theatrical expression of joy, although I failed to detect any undercurrent of unease. Her complexion was as smooth as polished stone. If it hid nothing, perhaps it was because there was nothing to hide. Mrs. Esterhazy was the empty space around which everything revolved, like water circling the drain.

To distract myself, I put on the radio set I'd bought the other day. Manne had had a liking for somber classical music, but Smith preferred jaunty jazz tunes, and I fiddled about to find a station that fit the bill. I'd looked away from the photo for only a minute or so, but that was all it took to break the spell. The image was no longer an instant of weird drama. It was just an ad again. I'd been so absorbed in my fantasy that I'd failed to observe the one thing that really mattered, the minuscule lettering along the left-hand side of the photo that said "Rigaut."

•

There was a back entrance to Stevenson's building. I knew that the door was sometimes left open for deliveries during the day, because I'd occasionally used it myself to avoid the doorman, back when Marie and I were still meeting at the apartment. It was locked now, but I managed to open it easily enough with a knife blade. I found myself in a steamy dark passageway, the walls wet as if sweating in the heat generated by the laundry, through an opening on the right. I could hear voices and the sound of machinery as I sneaked past, making my way up the stairs to the fifth floor. For a while I stood with my ear to Stevenson's door, until I was perfectly satisfied that no one was home. I took the key from under the carpet on the stairs, as I'd seen Marie do on past occasions, and opened the door.

The noise of traffic below was reduced to a dull hum, dampened by the heavy curtains that remained drawn. I'd been here enough times before, but never by myself, and there was a certain thrill to wandering around someone else's apartment without their knowledge. I was experiencing the space in a different way as well, seeing things I hadn't noticed before. In the sitting room, for example, it was now clear that one part of the ceiling was marginally higher than the other, and that the borderline corresponded to a difference on the ground as well: the floorboards on one side of the room were of a slightly different color to those of the other side. A wall must have at one time run through the room, I hypothesized. Perhaps it had originally been two studio rooms, joined together to make the two-bedroom apartment that it was now.

I found the phone book on the sideboard. I flicked through the *R* pages until I found Rigaut. The only nonresidential entry was for "Rigaut Images." Not an advertising firm, as I'd first supposed, but a photographic agency. It was located not far from where I was now, just beyond St. Patrick's on Madison.

I made the call and then wandered into the bedroom. There
again was the row of suits in the wardrobe—all seemingly
the same or with only minor variations—and a drawerful of
new white shirts. It occurred to me that I'd never seen this
man, nor his son; there was not even a photo of either in the
apartment. It was as if they existed on a different plane, which
could never intersect with mine. I took out one of his shirts
from the drawer and started to undress. Looking for cufflinks
I cast my eyes over to the dresser. Propped up against the mirror was a note, in fastidious handwriting.

> Darling I don't know if you'll drop by today. I'm in Bos-
> ton tonight but back tomorrow evening. I'll try to call.
> All my love

It didn't surprise me. I'd already imagined that Marie
and Stevenson were having an affair, probably long predat-
ing our own reconciliation. At the same time, I felt a shock
run through me. It's one thing to surmise that your lover is
sleeping with someone else; it's another to be presented with
the evidence. Without that, you can sort of believe and not
believe at the same time. You can still play the game that you
know your lover is also playing.

I didn't feel angry with Marie—why should I? I didn't even
feel angry with Stevenson. I thought back to the night Marie
and I had met at that bar on the Upper West Side. She'd been
more nervy then, physically more angular. She'd become more
confident in the following weeks: her body had changed too.
She was somehow more fleshy now, more overtly feminine.
I remembered going to bed with her for the first time. It had
been so completely different from Smith's previous sexual encounters, with the young women he'd meet in bars after work.
Those liaisons had been like a lighthearted game. With those

girls, there'd always be smiles and jokey banter in bed afterward: "Well, you certainly wanted that tonight, didn't you?" And we'd remain friends, bump into each other in other bars, maybe even go to bed together again. No, in some ways my relationship with Marie resembled more closely Manne's occasional affairs. But even then, there were differences. Manne's women tended to be difficult; there wasn't much sex involved, sometimes none at all. Marie wasn't like that. She had no hang-ups about sex.

I had one of Stevenson's suits on. I chose a tie and then went to the bathroom, where I found a compact, no doubt Marie's. I dabbed a little powder on my scar, which took the edge off it and softened the appearance of my face. I looked into the mirror and for a second had the impression that Manne was staring back. Funny how the simple fact of wearing a suit made you stand differently, see things differently. I went back to the bedroom and helped myself to some of the cash Stevenson had left on the bedside table, then jammed a few of his business cards into my coat pocket as well.

Madison Avenue was just a walk away. I went back out through the main entrance, sure that the doorman wouldn't stop me in my new clothes, even if he couldn't remember me ever going in. Stevenson would never realize that one of his suits was missing: that was how it was with men who bought the same of everything. But Marie would notice. I thought of her again. Only this morning I'd been contemplating the end of our affair with complete equanimity, and yet now I felt a sexual yearning, a sense of mourning for what couldn't be. I recalled that time Marie had taken me down to the Battery and we'd sat on the promenade looking out at the Statue of Liberty. She'd asked me then if I remembered when we'd last been there, just before I'd supposedly disappeared. Yes, I'd replied, and in a curious way I hadn't been lying, because the

affair took on a new reality in Marie's retelling. The haunting
nostalgia I'd felt had been all the more strange and powerful
precisely because I'd never been there previously with Marie.
I caught myself thinking of Abby, for the first time in a while.
My feelings for the two women were coming from the same
place, or perhaps merging from different places. Tears were
welling, and I stopped for a moment. Was Abby returning
because of Manne? Because I was back on the Esterhazy case?

I walked down Madison past the polished gold plates of
all the big names in advertising. I had this vision of a swanky
agency with its glass cubicles, clinical like a hospital, complete with an immaculately turned-out secretary, giving me
the brush-off. Instead, there was something decidedly furtive
about Rigaut Images. It was just a few rooms upstairs from
a jeweler's store, fronted by a middle-aged woman behind
a chaotic desk. As I waited to see the person I'd spoken to
on the phone, I took out the ad from my wallet. There they
were again: the man, the boy, Mrs. Esterhazy, frozen in their
moment of eternal expectation, like models in a museum. In
forbidding all movement, the photographer was a sort of taxi-
dermist, it struck me. The people captured inside the frame
were the animals, stuffed into dramatic poses. The more I
stared at the image, the more it seemed to be its own world,
referring to nothing outside itself, not even to the product it
was ostensibly promoting.

"Is that the one you're interested in?"

A Dickensian man in wire-rim glasses and a shabby jacket
was looking down at me.

"It's one of yours? I was wondering if I had the right place."

"You'd be surprised. We do quite a bit of work for the
slicks."

I followed him into a windowless office. One entire wall
was stacked with files, and as the man fiddled about trying

to locate the right one, he kept up a salesman's patter: "We're cheap, we're highly professional, and sometimes that's all an advertiser needs. We use stock images so we don't have the expense of setting up new shoots for each commission. When the shots are reused, we make sure they're for different markets. We can change their look through filters, removing or adding people or objects or backgrounds . . . here it is."

He'd pulled a file and opened it up on the desk between us. There was the picture again, in larger format, stripped of the text and slogan. There were other versions too, for different products, but all with the same shot—some in black and white, some with the husband or child cropped out, some with different color schemes. A half-dozen Mrs. Esterhazys smiled uncannily back at me.

"You've chosen a popular one. We've used it several times. What was your line of business again?"

"Insurance. Here's my card."

"I see. Managing director. Um. You deal with the advertising account as well?"

"Let me explain. I . . ."

"No need to explain, Mr. Stevenson. You told me you were interested in the female model, is that right?"

"That's right."

"Not the image per se."

"No."

The man put his elbows on the table, his hands under his chin, and stared at me.

"Well, there are various things we could do. We could of course draw up a contract right now for the use of the image. Or I could organize another shoot with the same model, if you're willing to pay. But I'm guessing that's not what you want."

"No."

"I'm afraid I can't simply give you her details. It wouldn't be acceptable."

"I'm aware of that. But perhaps if I . . ."

He stopped me with his hand. "I'll be frank with you, Mr. Stevenson. You're not the first person to get in touch with me like this. I'll tell you how we operate here. We don't use a modeling agency. It's more like a family. If I need Dora, I'll get her on the phone. If she's not free, maybe she'll recommend me someone, one of her young friends. That's the way it works. That's how I keep expenses down."

"Dora? Her name's Dora? Where's she from?"

"She's French, but she speaks perfect English. Now, I don't know what these girls get up to when they're not working for me. Most of them are trying to scrape a living together. Some of them don't have papers. It may well be that Dora would be perfectly happy to meet a gentleman for a drink. I can see that you're a gentleman."

"Tell me something more about her. Is she married? How long has she been here? What else does she do for a living?"

The man shook his head. "I'm afraid I can't really say anything more. What I'm willing to do, for a fee, is pass on your details to the girl in question. I'd be happy to do that. Now, what she does with them is none of my business. If she doesn't get in touch with you, then there's nothing I can do about that. There would be no point in coming back here. You do understand?"

"Yes. I do understand."

8

Darkness seemed to rise rather than fall. Thick snow blanketed the city, deadening the sound, the air curiously still. Few cars were risking the icy streets, and pedestrians moved slowly, silently, along the sidewalk, as if they were gliding just above it. Everything had been stripped of color, transformed to white-gray, and with the contrasting twilight shadows, you had the sensation of having wandered into an old photograph. I looked up at the skyscrapers, the lights pricking on one by one as if the buildings were gradually coming to life. I had the fleeting impression of seeing New York for the first time as it really was—an immense museum of strangeness.

I was outside Stevenson's apartment building again. I could see the light on, on the fifth floor. I'd told myself that I was coming back to return the suit I'd taken from Stevenson's wardrobe, but actually I knew it was about Marie. Not wanting to mess with the back entrance in the dark, I simply walked in through the front, with a cursory nod to the doorman's desk. He should have stopped me, had me wait until he'd called up to the apartment, but he didn't. Perhaps, I mused in the elevator, it was because I was wearing Stevenson's suit. Perhaps I resembled him now.

"Who's there?"

"It's me."

I could hear her fiddling around with the locks and then the door swung open. She had her hair up, and was wearing a bathrobe tied loosely at the waist, opened almost to her breasts. I could smell food cooking from the tiny kitchen.

"What are you doing? You shouldn't be coming around here."

"I wanted to see you. You weren't home."

"I never said I'd be home. I never said I'd be here. You shouldn't come around. Mr. Stevenson might have been here."

"But he isn't, is he?"

She went to turn off something on the stove, leaving me in the sitting room. Medical books were scattered about the floor, untidily piled up around a large notepad filled with a tiny scrawl. She'd been studying, lying on a cushion instead of sitting at the desk, obviously at ease in the apartment. I followed her through to the kitchen. She had her back to me. I put my arms around her waist under her bathrobe and kissed the nape of her neck.

"Come on. Let's go to the bedroom."

She didn't answer, but allowed me to lead her by the hand. I could feel a slight hesitation as I turned left in the corridor toward Stevenson's room instead of right to the boy's, where we'd slept together on previous occasions. She sat naked on the bed, her bathrobe at her feet, looking up at me almost quizzically. She must have just showered, as I could smell fresh soap on her, mixed in with her own perfume. I started kissing her, which again she let me do, without really responding. The passivity further stoked the tension building in me, and I undressed quickly. There was no resistance as I pushed her down onto the bed. For a minute or two she had her legs wrapped around me, but then she turned her face away from mine.

"No, stop. You're hurting me."

She was shifting underneath me. Without even noticing I'd had her arms pinned to the bed. Now I released them and took my weight off her. I lay beside her in a state of frustration. Eventually, Marie gathered up her bathrobe from the floor and wound it around her, pulling the cord tight. She pointed to the clothes I'd heaped on the chair by the desk.

"Why were you wearing his suit? How did you get it?"

"I needed it for a meeting. I knew there was a key outside under the carpet."

"Who were you meeting?"

"It doesn't matter."

"Doesn't matter? You think you can just walk in here and take his clothes? You could have at least asked me. What if he'd been here? Who were you meeting?"

"Too complicated to explain. Look, I . . ."

"Was it Dora Morel?"

"Dora? How do you know about her?"

Marie stared at me with pressed lips and then got off the bed. The mood, already ambivalent, had turned on a dime. I pulled on my clothes and followed her through to the kitchen, where she was stirring something steaming on the stove.

"How the hell do you know about her?"

"Are you seeing her? Is that it? Are you sleeping with her too?"

"I've never met her. I'm not sleeping with anyone else. Unlike you."

"What are you dreaming up now?"

"You and Stevenson. I'm not dumb."

"Don't be ridiculous. He already has a mistress."

"That's not true, is it? You're lying. You're lying to me!"

Marie turned around, and caught in her sudden movement, I pulled sharply at the lapels of her bathrobe. She yelped
and pushed back savagely at me. In surprise I let go, losing my
balance, my shoulder cracking hard against the sideboard. I
was flailing about trying to right myself, in a fog of pain, and
I reached out and grabbed the first thing that came to hand,
an almost empty whiskey bottle. As I spun to the floor, the
bottle caught the corner of a cupboard. A fine amber spray
spattered Marie's white bathrobe, like some sort of effluent.
The bottle hadn't shattered; the bottom had sheared right off,
in an almost perfectly clean break. I breathlessly got to my
feet, still holding what was left of the bottle.

"Put it down. Put that thing down!"

I was in shock, or perhaps I hadn't understood what she
was referring to. I froze as Marie dashed past me. She was
on the phone, talking with her hand over her mouth: "He's
threatening me with a broken bottle. Please come, please
come at once!" I let the bottle go; I didn't know why I hadn't
put it down. It bounced on the kitchen linoleum without
breaking any farther. At first I thought Marie had been calling
Stevenson, but then I realized that couldn't be the case, he was
in Boston. She was speaking to an operator, or the doorman,
or more probably the police.

I passed by a clock in a store window. It was a little after seven.
I couldn't have been at Stevenson's apartment more than a
half hour, although it felt much longer. Everything had happened very quickly and I was still reeling. It was minutes since
I'd left the building, but already my recall of what exactly had
happened was blurring. I'd lost Marie. I'd probably never see

her again. Not unless she came around in person to collect
her things. Perhaps she really was the one I wanted. I remembered the way I used to watch her as she lay on the bed, eyes
closed, breasts rising and falling with her breathing. Tears fell,
but all of a sudden they felt theatrical, and I wiped them away
with the back of my hand.

I was wandering down a typical midtown street—largely
empty, save for pockets of activity around the occasional bar
or restaurant. In my shock and tiredness, colors had taken on
a hallucinatory quality and the scene seemed secondhand. I
hadn't grown up in Manhattan. Even after years of living and
working there, it remained mythical. I'd be walking along,
I'd look up at a famous facade, and it would remind me of a
movie I'd seen, a postcard I'd sent, a book I'd read. Behind
the iconography was the real New York, whose secret life I'd
never know.

Under the haze of a streetlight I took out my wallet photo
of Marie. The old one from before the war, where she looked
so much younger, with different hair, in a thirties style. You
could almost imagine that it was someone else. It actually
brought back memories of the hospital, rather than of Marie
herself, as the photo had sat on my bedside table the whole
time I'd been there. But I stared at it for quite a while, all the
way to my station, trying to work out exactly what my emotions were. The sadness that had pierced me the moment I
knew Marie was lost, the feeling that she was the one I really
wanted—all that was already subsiding. It was a remnant of
Manne's way of thinking, his sense of romantic tragedy, of
only wanting what you can't have. Smith would take a more
pragmatic attitude. He'd be upset by events, no doubt, and
yet aware that life moves on. That there were plenty of other
opportunities for a man like him, in a city like New York.
That even tonight, if he wanted, he could go to a bar and find

someone to share his bed. Manne and Smith were both pas-
sionate and both cold—but in very different ways.

I didn't want to go home, didn't want to be alone in that
room, not yet. I found myself at the Public Library, half by
accident, half on purpose. Climbing the stairs to the impos-
ing entrance brought to mind the last time I'd been there,
some years before. It had been when I was researching the patient who had obsessively drawn pictures of a cityscape he'd
claimed had come to him in visions. And then, frustratingly,
I'd frightened him off with my heavy-handed tactics before
I'd worked out whether he was truly delusional—before, in
fact, I'd been able to help him at all. It was an unresolved case,
like so many others, but the one I'd always found peculiarly
poignant. I could still see the drawings in my mind's eye, of
a city unvisited and yet intimately known, perfect in its way.

That wasn't what had brought me to the library this time,
though. For some reason I'd wanted to see the paper Manne
had written on Miss Fregoli. It was the first case history I'd
had published, and perhaps the only piece I'd ever really been
happy with. If there were some key to Manne, I reasoned,
perhaps I'd find it there. I flipped through the cards in the
catalogue until I came to "Manne, David." Disappointingly,
there was no record of the Fregoli article. Although I must
have published at least a couple of dozen case histories, the
library listed only one. I went to the stacks and found it, in an
obscure university publication. I had no recall at all of writing this particular piece, although I certainly remembered the
case. A married man had left his family and had gone missing
for three months, only to return home one day, unable to remember where he'd been or what he'd done in the intervening
months. But after a month of intense therapy, I'd managed to
coax the details out of him. The fugue had been triggered by
the discovery of his wife's infidelity. He hadn't gone far; he'd

been living in a fleapit hotel only a few blocks from his house. By day, he'd keep watch on his family home. Sometimes he'd see his wife's lover enter or leave the house. Little by little, it seemed the lover was insinuating himself into the household, even to the extent of taking the kids to school occasionally. My patient told me that he'd felt he was peeking into some sort of alternative world, as he saw his wife and her lover arm in arm, off to eat at a favorite local restaurant.

I'd counted that case a success on my part, as I'd reached the root of the trauma and had banished the amnesia, but where had that left the patient? Had he reconciled with his wife? Was he any happier on account of my intervention? I didn't know, and perhaps had never known what had happened to him, nor was there any hint in the paper I'd written. It was a disturbing experience, reading a piece I couldn't even remember writing, and to my mind the author came off as pompous and obtuse. This was Manne as he'd presented himself to his academic audience, perhaps to his patients as well. It was a performance. Just one in a whole constellation of tiny performances that had made up his life. Wasn't that what anyone's life was, after all? A repertoire of roles, with no single guiding principle. There was also the Manne who had married Abby, for instance—surely a different creature. Now I was thinking about those early days after Abby's departure. The despair of returning to the unchanged apartment. The futility of washing up after a meal, or even cooking it in the first place. With no witnesses, you weren't really there at all.

I had another idea. I put the journal with my article back in the stack and went to the catalogue cards to look up Peter Untermeyer. No doubt he must have published something down the years. But when I checked, his record seemed almost as threadbare as Manne's. There was a longish article

summarizing the works of the Viennese psychologist, Otto
Rank. But only one paper of original work. It had been published soon after the war, at around the time I must have
bumped into him in Murray Hill. I could feel a mounting excitement as I found the piece in the bound copies of *Psychiatry
Today*, a prestigious journal that had never accepted a piece
of mine. I sat down to read it, but was quickly disappointed.
What Untermeyer was proclaiming to be a "revolutionary
new treatment method" for personality disorders seemed to
me merely an eccentric patchwork of notions, old and new,
taking in transference techniques, therapeutic identities, and
even at one point the "electromagnetic stimulation of the
brain." I was surprised that a reputable journal published the
piece, and skipped ahead to the concluding paragraphs. The
real shock was the biographical note tacked on to the end:
"Dr. Untermeyer fought with the Twelfth Infantry Regiment
in Europe, and subsequently headed a denazification unit in
occupied Germany. Since his return to the United States, he
has worked with the Stevens Institute in New York."

I scanned the vast reading room. Dozens of men, and a
few women, were crouched over their books, scribbling notes,
each in their own particular kingdom of exile. I glanced at the
big clock suspended above: it was now past ten o'clock in the
evening. Somehow, hours had passed by in the library. I was
not quite ready to go: galvanized by my discovery of the Untermeyer article and the biographical note, I opened the latest
issue of *Psychiatry Today*. I was wondering whether Dr. Peters
might have written about me, as I'd once suspected. Almost
at the same time as I had that idea, I noticed his name in the
contents list. It was difficult to shake off the powerful sensation that I'd willed it there myself, by merely thinking of it.
I found the page reference and ran my eye quickly over the
piece, until I came to this:

Case 4. S.S. is a white male in his midthirties, of no fixed profession or domicile. He had been brought to the emergency room with head injuries resulting from an attempted suicide in a subway station. While recovering from his injuries, S.S. acquired the strong delusional belief that he was a Park Avenue psychiatrist named Dr. M. This belief was of a direct transferred nature: a Dr. M. has offices at the address indicated by the patient, although he was on leave at the time of S.S.'s hospitalization. The patient presented typically for cases of monothematic delusional ideation: his thinking was observed to be well organized; he did not suffer from prominent or sustained hallucinations; there was little evidence of deterioration in mental functioning; there was no insight into his illness.

In the initial treatment period, standard Saltmeyer procedures were followed. The patient was kept in seclusion; he was interviewed daily; the delusion was not directly challenged. Under Saltmeyer, patients with good functional performance begin recovery within two to four weeks. This was not the case for S.S. In fact, repeated interviewing had seemed to harden his delusion into a complex, self-contained system with an additional paranoid dimension.

Approximately one month after the patient's admission, enhanced scenario (ES) technique therapy was attempted. The objective was twofold. It was hoped that a well-directed ES would trigger the psychic annihilation of the delusional persona, and secondly, that it would shift S.S.'s suicidal ideation onto the now discarded identity. An ES was developed to encompass both these objectives, while accommodating other elements of the patient's own psycho-ideational structure. S.S.'s

delusion was now bluntly challenged. He was told, in
brutal fashion, that the real Dr. M. had been traced, and
that he had recently committed suicide. S.S. greeted
this scenario with shock and bewilderment. There was
a brief period of resistance, which was eventually followed by a full recovery. Within two weeks, S.S. had
largely abandoned his delusional identity, and within
four weeks, he no longer mentioned Dr. M. at all.

There was quite a bit more, mostly theorizing, but I stopped
reading at that point—an immense fatigue had invaded me,
and I was too tired to concentrate. I contemplated tearing out
Dr. Peters's article and taking it with me, but then I realized
that I had no need to read any of it again. The case history
was much as I might have expected; I could have practically
written it myself. Dr. Peters had disappointed me: he'd gone
with the grain, offering up a story that fit too smoothly with
prevailing psychiatric practice—like a jigsaw piece sliding
perfectly into its place.

Back on the street, I picked my way through the drifting
snow. The cold had revived me a little. I mentally put Dr. Peters's piece of fiction to one side, although I knew I'd have
to examine its ramifications later. I was thinking about Mrs.
Esterhazy, as I still called her in my mind. I conjured up some
of the shadowy world in which I assumed she existed. She was
a refugee, perhaps, like Marie. She was making a buck in any
way she knew how. A little modeling work when it came her
way. Maybe some bit-part acting too. And she wasn't averse
to being taken out for a meal and a drink sometimes, maybe
more—after all, that's how Marie had probably met Stevenson. Then one day, through a demimonde contact, she'd

heard of a nice little job, earning her a hundred dollars for just a couple of hours' work. All she had to do was pretend to be someone's wife. She'd be given some kind of backstory, and told precisely what to say. It was all aboveboard. There'd even be a couple of cops there to prove it.

I played out that scene in my mind, and it seemed plausible enough. I thought about Untermeyer. That thumbnail biography linking him to the Stevens Institute was a cornerstone on which I could build the edifice of the Esterhazy case. I was sure that Dr. Peters had told me that the Stevens Institute didn't exist; I'd now found printed reference to it for the second time since my discharge. If I hadn't yet understood what had happened to Manne, at least it now seemed that an explanation was possible. At the same time, I suspected that once everything was clear to me, it would actually resolve nothing at all. That if I shone a light on that side of the problem, it would merely cast shadows on the other.

Once I reached home I was ready to collapse, nearly too exhausted to sleep. On the bed sat a scribbled note: "Miss Dora Morel called," and under that a number. The handwriting wasn't familiar, and for a minute or two I was flummoxed as to how this note could have found its way onto my bed. It seemed folded into a greater mystery, namely that of how Marie had known the name Dora Morel in the first place, before even I had learned the surname, and how she'd tied it in with me. In my tiredness it took me too long to arrive at the obvious, that the two mysteries dissolved when combined.

In the subway, I'd come to the conclusion that Marie must have known Dora Morel—perhaps they both moved in the same expatriate circles—and that, more improbably, Marie must have guessed a connection with me. Now I could clearly see that this was nonsense. Instead, Marie had come home, found the note shoved under my door, and put it on the

mattress. There was a phone in the hallway and the old lady—
the one I'd never seen—must have taken the call and written
the note. The corroborating evidence for this was that Marie's
things—her clothes and makeup—were all gone. She'd necessarily been here while I was out. Already, before I'd arrived
at Stevenson's apartment, she'd made her decision to leave
me. Whether it had been to do with the Dora Morel note, or
whether it had been around the corner anyway, there was no
way of knowing. Why then, I wondered, had she been ini-
tially prepared to have sex with me on my arrival? I dismissed
the question almost as soon as I'd formulated it. Behavior is
never more unstable than at the point of heightened emotion.
The most important thing was that Marie was always going to
leave. Faced with that inevitability, it was as if the affair had
never really happened in the first place.

I stretched out on the bed. My throbbing shoulder pre-
vented me from sleeping, for the moment at least. I could
hear the faint sound of barrel-organ music, drifting in from
somewhere—it was a funny hour for it. I was thinking not so
much of Marie now, and more about the Dora note. How two
mysteries could come together, and in so doing, annihilate
each other. Something like that was about to happen in the
Esterhazy case, what with the reappearance of Mrs. Esterhazy
and the proof of the Stevens Institute. The question was at
what cost. Would its resolution kill off Smith, entombing me
within Manne? I was determined that it would not.

9

There was one place to which I hadn't returned, not since the day I heard about Abby. I hadn't even so much as walked down Park Avenue since my discharge from the hospital. The idea of taking a look at my old office had come to me as I lay on my mattress, staring at the Rigaut photo pinned to the wall, unable to settle into anything else. I'd spent a feverish morning trying to speak to Dora Morel, calling her number at half-hourly intervals. No doubt she was out for the day, working, which meant there was no point in calling until the evening. But I couldn't stop myself obsessively dialing the number, and I knew that if I continued like that, my nerves would be completely shot by the end of the day. I had to get myself out of the apartment.

I climbed the subway stairs on East Seventy-Seventh, already picturing the short walk to my office. Every inch of that journey was burned onto my brain, every facade and storefront, every fire hydrant. Seconds before passing a building, I would have a mental image of it, and then moments later, compare it with the real thing. I was prepared for things to be different; it would have been normal that, in the months that had passed, a wall might have been repainted or demolished, a tree might have grown or died. But no: everything was the same.

Manne's apartment block had been redeveloped, the Stevens Institute destroyed: I could only wonder what might have happened to the Park Avenue building. The one thing that hadn't occurred to me was that it would be perfectly, preternaturally unchanged. The image of it, in sepulchral white stone, was a part of me, almost inside me. I walked past the entrance without stopping, but managed a quick glance at the brass nameplates lining one of the walls of the lobby. I had a sense that mine was still up there. There was a bench on the sidewalk, a couple of doors down. I'd walked past it a thousand times, but had never sat on it. No one ever did, apart from the occasional elderly man on return from his daily constitutional. But I sat down on it now, as it offered me a good view of my old building, without making it seem as if I were loitering.

I'd pretend to look elsewhere, but it was hard not to stare, watching the people as they came and went from the building, with greater frequency than I would have imagined. Many of them I didn't know, but some I recognized. They were the wealthy residents and their servants, who lived on the upper floors, and with whom I might have exchanged the occasional nod or pleasantry in the elevator. Contact had rarely gone beyond that, but by dint of repetition their faces would be forever there, lurking in the corners of my consciousness. They too were exactly the same, but insubstantial, ghosts, with no further relevance or existence in my life. And yet they lived on.

The experience of sitting and watching was intense and

boring at the same time. I didn't want to go into the building, for fear of being recognized. I'd returned to my former life, only to observe it from the outside in. I imagined Manne coming out from the lobby, and me watching him from my third-person perspective, as he wandered around the corner to a delicatessen, where he sometimes bought sandwiches to take to the Park. What had once been quite ordinary now transformed. All sorts of unrelated ideas came to me. I thought of the old lady who lived opposite me, whom I'd never seen or communicated with, and yet who must have taken the phone call from Dora Morel. And I thought of Dora Morel. I wondered whether I wanted to go to bed with her, as Marie had supposed. Perhaps Marie was right; perhaps I did. It was impossible to know who Dora was. When we'd met, she'd been the distraught wife of a supposed psychotic. In the magazine ad, she was the stereotypical American mother. The man at the agency implied that she was an illegal immigrant getting by on her good looks. The mask changed: it would change again should I ever meet her.

A man walked out of the lobby and stood by the curb, plainly waiting for a taxi. How many times had I done that myself? Judging from his appearance—the high polish on the shoes, the conservative, well-cut suit—he too might well be a doctor, with an office in the building, and although I vaguely recognized him, I couldn't place him. A cab pulled up. The man took off his hat and readied himself to get in. But then he seemed to change his mind and waved the taxi on. In the brief moment I'd seen him with his hat off, I knew who he was, with absolute clarity. The man I'd known as Esterhazy. He wasn't dead. He was there: tall, wiry, with dark eyes and that thick dark hair. He seemed to hesitate on the sidewalk, like an actor unsure of his lines. Then he set off down the avenue,

weaving his way randomly through the throng, as if he had
no particular destination in mind.

He wasn't hard to follow. The problem was to avoid over-
taking him, to keep back against the flow of people, because
his pace was that of a country stroll rather than a city stride. I
caught him looking up to the sky at one point, but most of the
time he had his hand to his chin, even while he walked, as if
deep in thought. Already we were in a stretch of Park Avenue
that I didn't know, had maybe never been down, despite the
fact that it was so close to where I'd spent a decade of my life.
We were in that hinterland between the two worlds of Manne,
that of his office and that of his apartment.

I'd quickly gotten the hang of the following game; I wasn't
going to lose Esterhazy. With the shock of seeing him reced-
ing, I found myself able to think, after a period in which my
brain had gone blank. Impossible to know what Esterhazy
was up to or where he was going; I'd just have to wait it out.
I was struck by how different he was from the last time I'd
seen him, comatose on my bed, pale, fragile, drugged. And
although I was certain that it was him I was following, there
was also a nagging voice in my head, reminding me that I'd
only seen him a couple of times before, many months ago, in
peculiar circumstances, so how could I possibly be so sure?
I supposed that he would eventually stop somewhere, and at
that moment, I might get a closer look.

I'd been following him an hour at least. After a while the
chase had become mesmerizing, my thoughts drifting off into
all sorts of random tangents. We'd gone all the way down Park
Avenue to Grand Central, and then the man had turned right,
in what had seemed an arbitrary manner. We were in one of
those anonymous midtown streets. He veered off the sidewalk, in such an abrupt fashion that I nearly lost him. He'd
walked into a bar, the kind of place that was nothing special,

with sawdust on the floor and a sprinkling of afternoon drinkers. Through the glass front I could see him talking to the barman, who promptly put a beer in front of him. My first thought had been to stay outside, but the reflections on the glass from the busy street made it difficult to see properly into the bar, and I was determined to get a better look at him.

Through the doors, everything felt different. After hours of people and traffic, of movement and noise, the place felt deathly still. The other patrons were for the most part immobile on their stools, staring into their drinks with a soulless determination. I frequented these kinds of bars myself, and although I was no alcoholic, I recognized the type. The unknowable men who would come in at ten in the morning, and stay there all day drinking in complete silence, only leaving when the after-work crowd eventually filtered in. Esterhazy, in his expensive suit and tie, looked wildly out of place. He'd downed his first beer quickly and had started on another. I climbed on a bar stool not far from him and ordered a whiskey. It was a reckless move, as he might easily have looked my way and recognized me. But I felt the need to scrutinize him at close quarters, to quiet the voice of doubt within me. Esterhazy paid me no heed, in any case. There was a flickering intensity to his eyes as he gazed out through the glass front into the streetscape, its somber colors more redolent of fall than the beginnings of spring after a bitter winter.

It was Esterhazy all right. I couldn't doubt it now. He hadn't died in my bed, as I'd been led to believe. Dr. Peters had admitted as much, in the case history I'd looked at in the library. I tried to spin out a story that would account for Esterhazy's sudden reappearance. I cast my mind back to the day I'd seen him for the last time, lying comatose in my bedroom. I'd left him there, after Mrs. Esterhazy's phone call. Some time later, he would have woken up. Alone, in a strange room, wearing strange clothes. His mind still hazy from the coma, he would have no recall of my visit to him at the Stevens Institute, of the taxi ride home, of my practically carrying him up the stairs to my apartment. No, instead he would have felt the bizarre shock of waking up, only to find that he was in fact some-one else. Hesitatingly, he gets out of the bed and goes to the other room, to see if he recognizes anything in it. He stares out the window, to a blank wall opposite. Eventually he makes his way to the bathroom. There on the shelf, sitting next to a water glass and a toothbrush, he sees a wallet. His wallet, no doubt. He opens it and finds a driving license in the name of Dr. David Manne. Business cards too, with an address on Park Avenue. And now he walks to the front door. By the en-trance is a small table, on which lies a key. His key.

Esterhazy was beside me. From the corner of my eye I watched him as he sat there wordlessly for twenty minutes or so, sipping at his beer from time to time, in a sort of reverie. But then when the bar started to fill up with the first wave of workers, the ambience changed. As abruptly as he'd entered the bar, Esterhazy now left it, slapping a dollar bill down on the bar beside his empty glass. Again he seemed to pause out-side, as if uncertain which way to go, before turning left onto Sixth Avenue.

He hadn't quickened his meandering pace, but for long moments now I lost sight of him, in the chaotic rush of peo-ple on their way home. He was heading north; his movements seemed to describe a huge circle, and I wondered whether he was returning to where he'd started. If that were the case, then what was the purpose of this long ramble? Esterhazy stopped momentarily by a phone booth, as if about to make a call, but then moved on again. The whole journey was like this, punc-tuated with small hesitations.

It was twilight, the enigmatic hour, so often lost in the New

York rush. We'd reached the end of the Avenue, and Central Park stretched out before us like an ocean. But Esterhazy didn't too venture too far in, settling for a bench overlooking the Pond on the south side. We were away from the sidewalk crowds now, and relatively few people were in the Park this late in the day. I watched the geese gliding effortlessly across the water and felt my muscles relax: I couldn't lose him here. I found my own bench a good fifty yards from his, so that I could just see his dark head, and I'd be alerted easily enough when he moved off. What was the meaning of his long meander? Throughout this whole affair, I'd always assumed that he was the principal victim. That he'd been drugged, then committed under false pretenses. And that what had happened to me was simply part of that wider picture. Now, I wasn't sure of that at all.

I gazed up into the graying skies, pulling my eyes away from Esterhazy for the first time since the bar. Great dark clouds of birds swooped and wheeled high above. At one point they appeared to be moving backward en masse, no doubt an optical illusion. It was ominously beautiful, and illustrated something a patient had once pronounced out of the blue: "We come from a place where the birds fly backward." I'd paid no heed at the time, but the words spooked me now. For a few minutes, ever-greater concentrations of birds filled the sky, swirling around until in one seemingly synchronized movement, they headed south and out of sight.

Esterhazy was up again. He'd only been on the bench for ten minutes or so, and I guessed he'd wanted to move on before it became too dark. I trailed him as he headed east out of the Park, then crossed Fifth and Madison. I'd been right, he was going back to the starting point. We were on Park Avenue, a block or so from the building, when Esterhazy suddenly spun around. Instinctively I threw myself into a doorway. I waited out an excruciating ten seconds. When I poked my head around the corner, the fedora pushed down almost to my eyes, I caught Esterhazy just as he was turning back. He'd clearly stood there a good moment before deciding to walk on. Had he seen me? In any case he'd had an intuition that he was being followed. It shook me up and I hung back a bit until I saw him finally ducking into the building, giving a quick nod to the doorman, as if at least they were acquainted with each other. I sat down again at the bench near the entrance.

It was quite dark now, cold too. I wouldn't actually be able to sit it out for too long, I realized; I'd freeze to death. I felt a crushing tiredness from the long walk, the whiskey, the lack of anything to eat. But I was also in a febrile state of mind, buzzing from the events of the day. I put my hands in my pockets to keep them warm. I could feel the piece of paper I'd shoved deep into one of them, the one with Dora Morel's number. Over the long afternoon of tailing Esterhazy, I'd put his "wife" out of my mind. I cast my eyes down the avenue in search of a phone booth, but there wasn't one. It was Friday evening, in any case. Dora Morel was an attractive young woman; she was probably out somewhere. I had her image in my mind now, her neat figure, and I was wondering what it would be like to see her naked, to feel her body, to go to bed with her. I swung around, my heart pumping. I, too, had suddenly had the unnerving feeling that someone was stalking me. I strained to make out anything in the blackness.

An elderly woman in a heavy fur coat emerged from the lobby. Just behind her was Esterhazy. He could barely have had time enough to go up in the elevator and come down again. Someone was accompanying him, a man in a uniform wearing a cap, probably a police officer but it was hard to see in the dark. The two were in conversation, and the way they were interacting suggested that no coercion was involved, that it was a relationship of equals. With a thrill I realized that they were heading my way, were going to walk straight past where I was sitting. "We'll be outta there in a half hour, forty minutes, then you're free," the police officer was saying. I recognized the voice, but I didn't dare look up until they passed. I recognized the loping gait as well; it was exactly the same as when we'd been teenagers together, out on Long Island. Esterhazy was with D'Angelo. It was a moment of extraordinary intensity. They rounded the corner, and I jumped up from the bench. Although I hardly wanted to draw attention to myself, I couldn't help racing toward them. Esterhazy was climbing into the passenger seat of a police car, the two of them still in conversation. I had the impression that he'd glanced my way, just for a tiny moment, as if in an obscure acknowledgement of something. Before I had time to understand what was happening, the car roared off and disappeared into the traffic, fluid at that hour. Within seconds I'd lost sight of it. I'd been trailing Esterhazy the entire afternoon, and he was gone in an instant.

I stood on the corner, staring after the car, long after it had swept down the dark avenue. It had been heading south, and I chewed over that fact for a minute or two, but in the end could surmise nothing in particular from it. To get out of this part of town, a vehicle could only realistically go north or south. I continued peering down the avenue, though, as if I might spot something important if only I looked hard enough. On every corner of every Manhattan street were those canyon-like vistas, where you could see forever down a straight line to a vanishing point, like a lesson in perspective.

I was in turmoil: deflated that I'd lost Esterhazy, exhilarated that I'd seen him with D'Angelo. I was invaded with the feeling that I'd already solved the Esterhazy case—not in

its particulars, but that I'd divined the essence of its structure. The connection between Esterhazy and D'Angelo I'd
seen with my own eyes; I had documentary evidence of the
connection between Untermeyer and the Stevens Institute.
Bridging these two relationships was my own experience in
the hospital, and the mysterious visit from Untermeyer. It
was a structure that could generate only a limited number of
stories. It almost didn't matter which I chose.

10

I'd come early. Even so, I was too late. I'd wanted to be there
before she arrived, but I could see Dora Morel through the
glass front of the bar, dressed stylishly, sitting in the very same
booth that Marie and I had shared months before. A waiter
passed by and bent down toward her. She looked his way momentarily but then shook her head and said something very
quickly. The waiter shrugged his shoulders and moved on.
Even without hearing it I could interpret the exchange well
enough. We'd made a date, but she was going to wait until I
was actually there before getting a drink, in case I didn't show
and she wound up having to pay for it. I didn't resent her for
that, but I hesitated before going into the bar. For a moment
the glass that separated us seemed like a screen, as if I were
watching a scene from a movie that I was about to enter. It
was a mirror too, projecting my own faint image back onto
me. Hair combed and slicked back, wearing Stevenson's smart
dark jacket, I looked like neither Manne nor Smith, but an ap-
parition hovering between the two.

"Miss Morel?"

"So you're the mystery man."

I took off my hat and sat down opposite her. As always, I felt exposed bareheaded, with nothing to pull down to hide my face when I felt the need. I was aware of her looking me up and down, but I didn't note any particular reaction to my scar in her frank gaze—not the tiny, involuntary wince I sometimes detected in people I'd just met. No hint of recognition, either.

"What'll you have? What do you say we get a couple of martinis?"

"Swell. You know what? Are you hungry at all? I haven't had a thing since breakfast."

"Sure. Let's eat. They say the steak is good here."

In fact I wasn't hungry, but it might have made her uncomfortable to dine alone. I complimented her on her appearance; as we waited for the food the small talk flowed effortlessly, as if from a banal script that we'd already been over together. No mention was made of the circumstances of our meeting. We were playacting a date, when of course we both knew it wasn't that. I imagined the Dickensian man from the agency calling her up: "Strange thing happened this afternoon. Big-shot businessman drops by the studio. Pulls out that *Look* spread you did from his pocket, asks who you are. Long story short, he's fallen for you and wants to meet you! Good for a meal at least I'd say. That's if you want to take the chance . . ."

"Tell me a bit about yourself."

"Not much to say. Just a girl trying to make a living in the city. I do some modeling and take some acting classes. Guess I'm trying to break into the theater."

"You're French, right?"

"Ah . . . my father's French, yeah."

She didn't look it or sound it. I doubted Dora Morel was her actual name anyway—it was too mellifluous to be real. There was something exaggerated about her, from the circumflex eyebrows to the provocative strapless gown that was a touch too dressy for the place. Even the way she held her cigarette seemed too self-conscious, as if she'd only just learned to smoke. I could see the look she was aiming at: a cross between a movie starlet, and the femme fatale such a starlet might play. But while her Mrs. Esterhazy had been consummate, her Dora Morel seemed less assured.

"And what about you?"

"What do you want to know? I'm in business. Been in insurance all my working life. I've got a young son, he's the other love of my life. Sometimes he's with me, sometimes he's with his mother, across the river."

"You're divorced?"

"Amicably. She's over in Park Slope. I'm in Sutton Place . . ."

The date patter came to me easily enough. It wasn't strained, the way Manne would have done it, to ratchet up the intensity. It was more in Smith's style, if Smith had been a career professional, more smoothly urbane, more practiced at putting the other person at ease. As I conjured up the details of Stevenson's life for her, they took on a subjective reality—believing in my own performance was somehow necessary to it being a good one. No doubt that was true for Dora Morel as well. And perhaps her act was more subtle than I'd first given her credit for. In fact, she wasn't playing a femme fatale badly. Rather, she was doing a fine job playing a would-be actress playing a femme fatale badly. A young woman, sitting alone nearby, got up and left. As she swept past our table, I thought I caught fleeting eye contact between her and Dora Morel. Probably a friend Dora had gotten to keep an eye on her: "Got a blind date with this guy. May turn out weird. If you can be there when he comes, then I'll give you a signal when I know it's all right."

I'd been talking about Stevenson's lakeside home upstate, about the canoeing there in midsummer. We'd finished the steaks; Dora had ordered a desert. There was a tiny break in the conversation, a moment of perfect balance. We could be nearing the end of the evening. In the next twenty minutes, I could be paying the check, helping her with her coat, walking her home or finding her a taxi . . .

"There's a movie theater just around the corner, on Broadway. If you like, we could probably make the nine o'clock session . . ."

"That's a great idea," she replied.

I watched her as she ate her chocolate cake. The fact that I hadn't ordered a desert, and that she'd gone ahead anyway, underlined the relationship. She'd played it close to her chest. She'd talked enough about herself, and yet there was almost nothing to hold onto. An hour in her company, and I still didn't know where she'd come from, where she lived, any particular detail that would have individualized her, distinguished her from the thousands of other pretty young women one saw every day on the streets of Manhattan. In fact, this very lack of particularity distinguished her. The one constant, from Mrs. Esterhazy to Dora Morel, was her accent, which seemed to come from nowhere.

It was only a five-minute walk to the theater. On the way there, as we crossed the street, I touched Dora's lower arm in a way that was an invitation for her to seek out my hand, and when she did, I instantly knew that she meant to sleep with me that night. I got tickets and we found seats up at the back, just as the newsreel began to roll. Something was up with it, but it took me and the rest of the audience a few minutes to realize that. The wrong newsreel had been put on. This one was years out of date. There were stock shots of Nazis, and Berlin prior to its destruction, bustling with crowds. Eventually people in the movie theater began to laugh, then boo when images of Stalin, backed with friendly commentary, came on. The lights went up, the reel was stopped and replaced. I'd bought tickets to the latest Hitchcock, but there were a couple of movies screening. We must have accidently walked into the wrong one, because what we ended up seeing was a mediocre weepie, about a showgirl who falls in love with a returned war veteran. A date picture, in other words. As the characters flickered across the screen, Dora rested her head on my shoulder and I put my arm around her. I wanted her, or perhaps Stevenson wanted her. Because Smith was surely after something else.

We didn't talk afterward; we wandered dreamily through streets that were fairly empty even on a Saturday night, this being a quiet corner of the Upper West Side. We passed by a cheap hotel I'd once taken Marie to. I asked Dora if she wanted a last drink in the bar downstairs, and she nodded. But once we were inside, a jazz band started up, making conversation pretty much impossible.

"Let's rent a room for an hour and get the drinks sent up."

We signed in and made our way upstairs. The room was clean enough but simple and functional, just a bed, a couple of chairs and table, a single print on the wall by way of concession to decoration. Minutes later a bellhop arrived with a couple of glasses and some whiskey. I wondered whether Dora would think it strange, going to this slightly seedy hotel, when I was a wealthy, divorced insurance executive with my own apartment. Of course, she'd never have believed that story in the first place. I wasn't divorced. My wife was probably waiting for me in the Sutton Place apartment. And we couldn't go anywhere more salubrious, in case I was recognized.

She'd gotten out of her dress and was in her underwear, drinking whiskey. I put my arms around her and we kissed for a while, but it wasn't working. We stopped for a moment, sat down on the bed together and drank more whiskey. I wasn't sure what was bothering me. I hadn't drawn the curtains and through the window I could see into another hotel room opposite. It, too, was occupied by a man and a woman, in all likelihood about to go to bed together, the woman also in her underwear.

"Do you like your work? Do you enjoy modeling?"

"It's easy money. I don't want to do it forever."

"What about acting?"

"I like it better. It's what I want to do."

"Did you ever get asked to do something out of the ordinary?"

"Like what?"

"Like, maybe impersonate someone."

"Don't know what you're getting at."

"I mean, get paid to pretend you're someone else, to fool someone."

"Um, no I don't think so."

"You're sure about that? You never worked for the police? You never . . ."

"Entrapment? No. I don't know why you're asking me all these questions. Is this some game?"

I could see the change in her face, from one moment to the next. I could see her decide that she was a whole lot less sure of me after all. In fact she was eyeing her dress on the floor, transparently wondering whether she could reach down for it and put it back on without upsetting me.

I'd played it all wrong. There'd been no hurry, and yet I'd hurried into it. We could have finished the evening pleasantly; we could have dated over several more evenings; we could have settled into a comfortable pattern, until I was sure she trusted me. But there was no way I could reel it all back in now.

"Esterhazy. Does that name mean anything to you?"

"Ester-what? I don't know. Tell me exactly what you want from me."

The atmosphere had turned chilly. I could feel another Dora coming through, another mask. There'd been the case— it had been all over the papers—of the so-called "hotel killer," a charmer who had asked out girls, took them to cheap hotels, then strangled them and made off down the fire escape. Perhaps Dora had read about it. I was tempted to say something about it, to reassure her, but then I realized it would only make things worse. I pressed on.

"A man named Esterhazy. Lying on a mattress, probably drugged. You were playing his wife. In an apartment, somewhere downtown, Lower East Side. The police were there. I was there. You must remember it."

"I don't do entrapments. I don't do drug busts. I don't do the wayward husband stuff. Or anything like it."

"I don't know what story they fed you. I was there, and we talked, don't you remember?"

"I don't remember."

"You must. Last year, you must remember, think about it, think, think, *think!*"

She was staring at me wide-eyed. In my agitation I'd stood up, but then immediately realized that it could be taken for a menacing gesture, and so I sat down again without moving from the spot. It must have looked like a bizarre thing to do, and if it didn't break the tension, it somehow changed the power dynamic. In any case, it emboldened Dora to get up and retrieve her dress. As she pulled on her clothes she started gabbling, the words spilling over each other. Her hands were barely trembling, but they were trembling nonetheless.

"I don't know. Who knows? I may have done something like that. I don't know. I couldn't tell you the details, I don't remember. I have no recall. People ask me to do all kinds of crazy things. There you go. But I gotta go. Thanks for the great evening. Thank you. Now I gotta go."

"Wait. Wait!"

I could have physically stopped her. I could have frightened her enough for her to have told me whatever I wanted. Her footsteps echoed up from the stairwell and I looked around the hotel room. The impression of her body on the bed was still apparent; a twisted, lipsticked butt was smoking in the ashtray. I looked out the window to the hotel room opposite, but its light was now out.

II

Sunday morning. I lay in bed an hour longer that usual, feeling neither tired nor well rested. As I stared at the picture of Doral Morel pinned to the wall, the events of the previous night came back with a hallucinatory intensity. There was a gnawing feeling that I wouldn't be here in this apartment much longer, a few days at the most. I imagined the landlord from the agency banging on the door and then forcibly entering, after he hadn't received the month's rent. Magazines stacked about the place, dirty clothes in a basket, a half-empty tin of coffee, a business card, a book opened on a certain page. Why were things as they were? Why had I kept this and not that? I cast about for anything of Marie's, any evidence that she'd stayed here, but could find none.

It was a cold, crisp, bright day. The sun seemed directly above the city, its light allowing no shadows. I went out onto the street without any particular destination in mind. Lately I'd been doing this a lot, spending my days wandering the city, restlessly seeking some sort of stillness in motion. Images from the night before continued to replay in my mind. The shots of wartime Berlin from the wrong newsreel superimposed themselves on the streets before me. That city was gone, it no longer existed—I'd seen the photos of Berlin's ruin, mile upon mile of rubble. Cities seemed solid, dependable things, their landmarks fixed points on the landscape. In reality, they were as transient as the wind. I passed a blind man with his white stick. He wasn't wearing the normal dark glasses and I could see his dead eyes, completely white, as if they'd entirely swiveled around and were staring inward.

I was back outside my old apartment building. It had changed again. In the months since I'd last been there, it had been remodeled and renovated. Other buildings in the block had gone the same way, yet others were empty shells. A tenement building had been torn down, and on the juxtaposing wall you could see a chessboard of different colored wallpapering, belonging to the different rooms that had once occupied the space.

I walked to the corner where Manne's regular diner had been. It was closed, cocooned in boarding, waiting to be transformed into something else—an upmarket restaurant perhaps, or a luxury goods store. I had an image in my mind of the table I'd always sat at, with its idiosyncratic cracks and scratches on the white top that over the years had faded to cream. What had happened to the waitress, I wondered. She'd been there longer than I had, at least a decade. Had she been thrown out of a job from one day to the next, forced into another, less certain life? Somehow, if the diner no longer existed, then she no longer existed either. She'd melted away, like paper in the rain. In a few years, or perhaps only a few months, this whole quarter, Manne's neighborhood, would be completely unrecognizable, any trace of Manne's former existence there expunged.

Esterhazy strode out through the gates of my old apartment building. Even if my heart jolted painfully against my ribcage, I felt no real shock. I'd almost been expecting him. There was an unfathomable logic to his reappearance: I'd seen him at my old office building, and now I was seeing him at my old apartment building. I wasn't panicked about following him; I'd done it before and knew I could do it again. Nonetheless, he'd taken off at a fair pace, weaving purposefully through the Sunday crowds—it was clear that this time around, he actually had somewhere to go. Remembering the occasion when he'd spun around, obviously suspecting someone was following him, I kept a discreet distance. But at a crossing, as he waited for the green "walk" signal, I managed to get a good look at him. Hatless, hair neatly combed, he was dressed in beige pants with jacket and tie—the typical Sunday attire of a professional man. Esterhazy stared across the street at nothing in particular, his eyes never wavering, as if in deep reflection. The lights changed and he took off across the street, moving frictionlessly through the city as if in a dream.

At Fifty-First and Lexington, he ducked into the subway. During the week, I might have lost him in the crowds, but today the station was relatively deserted. I followed him through the turnstiles as he climbed down the stairs and waited on the platform for a southbound E train. I was fairly close to him now, closer than I ideally wanted to be, but I had to be in the same car so that I'd know when he got out. I looked in front of me, occasionally stealing glimpses of Esterhazy. He'd lost the thousand-yard stare now and seemed fidgety. He took out a packet of Lucky Strikes and lit one up, despite the fact that a train was due any moment and the cigarette would necessarily be wasted. It was the kind of thing that either Smith or Manne might have done—a rare point of intersection between the two. As I watched him smoke, I considered approaching him and asking for a light. Perhaps a conversation would ensue; perhaps he might even recognize me. It would trigger something, but to what end? I hadn't understood Esterhazy's role, or even why I was following him. For a long time I'd supposed him to be the primary victim, my own troubles were a mere consequence of the machinations that had led to Esterhazy's committal. Now, I wondered if that were true. We'd switched places. Somehow, he'd slipped into my life, just as I'd slipped into his.

The train pulled in; Esterhazy threw his cigarette to the ground after barely a couple of puffs. I followed him into the car and sat a few seats down from him. I wished I'd brought something to bury my head in, a newspaper or book. Instead, I was reduced to stupidly staring ahead again, at an advertisement for hair dye, complete with before and after photos of a mousy girl metamorphosed into a sexy blonde. If Esterhazy had turned my way he'd have gotten a good solid look at my face. Fortunately, he at least had brought some reading matter with him, typed sheets he'd extracted from a folder under his arm. He seemed to be absently shuffling through the pages, not really concentrating on them, but unable or unwilling to pull away from them either. Sneaking a sideways glance, I strained to make out anything of them, even just to decipher a word. But all I could discern was the form, the neat paragraph blocks with headings, and the flow of the text that was continually interrupted by what looked to be superscript numbers, presumably for footnotes. What he was reading was probably an academic or scientific paper. Was he the author? Or was I? We were stopped at a station, and for a moment, I contemplated snatching the pages out of his hands and racing out of the car doors. I remembered the thrill I'd felt on discovering the paper by Untermeyer at the library, followed by the deflation on actually reading it. The doors snapped shut, the train lurched forward, and the moment for action passed.

A few stations later, Esterhazy straightened the papers, put them back in the folder, and got up from his seat. We were at Penn Station. He was going to meet someone arriving by train. We climbed the stairs that led directly to the main concourse, frighteningly immense after the confines of subway tunnels. Esterhazy seemed momentarily lost in the vastness of the space, then he walked over to the departures and arrivals board and stared up. My thoughts jolted forward. Already I was envisaging an Esterhazy pacing the platform as a train eased its way in and slowly came to a halt. A door opens and an elegantly dressed woman, laden with baggage, steps down from the front car. Esterhazy calls to a porter, before striding over to embrace the woman. I see her face over Esterhazy's shoulder and it is that of Dora Morel. It's a world in which Dora actually is who she once pretended to be. Surely such a world did actually exist, in some unattainable fashion.

I gazed at the station's greenhouse roof high above as the noonday sunshine filtered in, spliced by the arched steel frame into a complicated game of light and shadow. It transfixed me for a moment, then I looked back down to see Esterhazy walking briskly over to the ticket counters and joining a queue. I'd gotten it wrong. He wasn't meeting a train, he was getting one. The fact that he had no luggage or even a briefcase with him had fooled me. I too joined the queue, a half-dozen people behind him. A vague plan had hatched in my mind: I would watch which platform he went to, work out from that which train he was catching, and buy my ticket. The queue was moving quickly enough and Esterhazy was at the counter now, negotiating with the clerk. He took a bill out of his wallet and the clerk slipped him his ticket and change under the glass. Glancing briefly up at the big clock that hovered over the concourse, Esterhazy broke into a light trot. People were hustling onto an LIRR train that, according to the indicator, was bound for Queens and suburbs beyond. Esterhazy bounded down the stairs onto the platform and slipped into the last car, seconds before the whistle blew and the doors slammed shut. The whole action, from the ticket counter to the train, seemed so fluid—as if it had been rehearsed.

I'd made my way to the front of the queue, and the clerk was looking at me questioningly.

"Sorry. I've changed my mind."

No point in getting a ticket now; I had no idea where Esterhazy might get off. I stood there a minute or so, staring after the train, and then wandered out a side entrance onto the street. Was it still morning? Days would pass in seconds, seconds in days: time was strange alchemy. I was hungry now and instinctively made my way to an old H&H Automat around the corner, where I'd used go to with my aunt and uncle as a boy. Surprisingly, it was still there, physically unchanged. It had always been our first port of call, straight off the train: my aunt and uncle would get coffee and a Danish before we set out for the big stores. Back then, that visit to the Automat had excited me, had defined the gleaming modernity of the city against the dull semirural suburb I'd grown up in. Now I put my coin in and took out an unreal-looking pie from behind a scuffed window. As I bit into it, I was thinking about Esterhazy. It had occurred to me that since he hadn't had a bag with him, and since he'd only taken a suburban train, he would probably be back in the afternoon or early evening. If I hung around at the station, I might well see him again.

At a loss what to do with myself, I killed time wandering slowly up to Bryant Park and then back again. Esterhazy was never far from my thoughts. I imagined him on the day of my subway accident, in my apartment, taking off my pajamas, pulling on a shirt and pants from my wardrobe, then disappearing into Manhattan in a daze of confusion. Perhaps he, too, had met with some kind of accident, and had found himself in a hospital emergency room. Perhaps the doctors there had discovered my wallet in his pocket, and had drawn their own conclusions.

Eventually, I found myself once more at Penn Station. The concourse was far from empty—every few minutes a new wave of passengers would stream up the stairs from the platforms, returning from their weekend away—but it wasn't teeming either, as it would have been on any other day but Sunday. If Esterhazy were returning today, I stood a good enough chance of seeing him. I bought a newspaper and positioned myself by the great columns at the entrance of the waiting room, giving me a good overall view of the LIRR platforms.

Impossible to read the newspaper. Instead I let my eyes flit randomly around the station, watching the people as they came and went, hauling luggage behind them or racing down the steps as Esterhazy had done. There was a certain sadness inherent to train stations. Not because they set the scene for tearful farewells, but because they were nonplaces, dead spaces. No one lived there, no one did anything there but pass through, from one point in the past to another in the future. Often, when forced to wait at a station, I would look at the people and invent little stories for them—the suave, middle-aged gentleman embracing a young woman, for example: is he taking his niece out to lunch, or has he come into the city for a tryst with his mistress? But this time I didn't do that. As the people before me went about their business, they seemed mere facades, automatons with no apparent motive or inner existence. Perhaps it was the station's monumental architecture that crushed those caught within it, bleeding them of their subjectivity. And yet the station's pillars and vaulting arches were themselves a fraud, no more real than a Hollywood set for a silent movie.

I saw him. I hadn't noticed him getting off the train. I surely would have missed him altogether, if I hadn't felt someone staring at me. I looked up, and there he was, a good twenty yards away. I hid my face again behind the newspaper, but too late. He'd clearly caught sight of me, had somehow been aware that I'd been waiting for him. I froze, waiting for Esterhazy to make his move. For a moment, I thought he was going to confront me. Perhaps that was even what I wanted, to force the game one way or another. But in the end he turned around and went to a phone booth just off the concourse. From my vantage point I could still see him pretty well, there was no need to move. He picked up the receiver and spoke briefly. It was all over in less than a minute. What was it about? Was he reporting my presence to someone? It seemed like that, because when he came out of the booth, he deliberately looked my way again, before glancing up at the big clock. I found myself mimicking him, looking up at the clock as well. It was nearly five. Hours had passed, when I could have sworn that it was minutes.

Esterhazy was heading back into the subway. At the risk of losing him, I held back. If I followed immediately, it would be too obvious. Not that he didn't already know that I was trailing him, of course. But made manifest like that, there would have to be public recognition of the fact. As things stood now, I could continue playacting, pretending to read my newspaper, and he could continue pretending that he wasn't being followed. Finally, a few minutes later, I, too, made my way into the subway. My thinking was that with a bit of luck, a train wouldn't have come yet and he'd still be on the platform—I could only suppose that since he'd taken a southbound E train to the station, he'd be taking a northbound one back. But when I rounded the corner before the turnstiles, there he was. He hadn't gone down to the platform. He'd been waiting for me. Instinctively I pushed my hat lower over my head— although it was far too late for that—and quickened my pace. I was through the turnstiles and continued down the tunnel. I didn't dare turn around to see if he were there, but I imagined not. Esterhazy had played me well, had shaken me off. He'd probably gone back up to the concourse and found a different way to continue his journey. I'd lost him, this time for good.

12

The light filtered through the grime of the windowpane and into my eyes. I sat bolt upright. I'd been having a nightmare. I'd died in my dream; I'd felt the life ripped out of me, and it had been painful and terrifying. I'd heard a low, distorted voice speaking to me as the breath had flown out of my chest, and then I'd woken up. I was shaking, slimy with sweat despite the freezing temperatures. I got off the mattress in search of a cigarette, in an effort to calm myself down. The silence, the absolute silence, unnerved me as I fumbled about with a café matchbook. I looked back to the mattress where I'd been lying a moment before, and couldn't help but imagine myself still there, dead as in my dream, arms by my side as if a mortician had already laid me out.

The nightmare had left me with a horrible sense of foreboding that was hard to shake. I looked about the sparsely furnished room. My premonition about not being here for much longer felt more right than ever—indeed, something to act upon. The few things that lay about the place seemed to have an elegiac aura to them. Again the sound of barrel-organ music, borne on the wind and modulated by it, wafted into the apartment. I smoked a cigarette, and then I smoked another. Out on the landing, the phone was ringing, on and on, like a tolling bell. It cut out after a few minutes, but then immediately started up again. Perhaps it was for me. In fact, it probably was. No one else seemed to be in the building now, except the old woman across the landing.

I showered and dressed in minutes. Pulling on my pants, I noticed my wallet sitting by the sink. I took out the photo of Marie, the same one that had sat on my bedside table in the hospital. Dora's photo remained pinned to the wall. I recalled other photos. The one of my father, looking so much like myself behind the walrus mustache. Or the one D'Angelo had given me, of an impossibly youthful Abby. The silky surfaces of these images were formaldehyde, fixing possibility to a moment, killing what was portrayed. People trapped within them would remain forever haunted by their own futures. I left Marie's photo on the table and stuffed the wallet into my pocket.

I wouldn't be back. Nevertheless, and for no good reason, I slipped the key under the carpet on the stairs after I'd slammed the door shut for the last time. Not a sound now that the phone had fallen silent. Outside on the railings by the stoop, someone had tied a large, official-looking sign. The building was going to be demolished, it said. In fact, the whole street was to go. It had been bought up by the city as part of a slum clearance plan, and new public housing would be built on the site. It wasn't much of a surprise: where the other streets around and about were crowded and bustling with life, this one had always had a ghostly quality, a vague feeling of desolation as if the very stones knew that their time was up. I'd been scammed, no doubt, into paying rent on an apartment that had already been abandoned, sold up, marked down for demolition. I could have kicked down the door and lived there for free. It seemed that Smith's universe—its streets, flophouses, bars, and docks—was now disappearing as quickly as Manne's. As if I'd deliberately been released from the hospital just in time to observe its extinction. Smith, like Manne before him, was losing shape and form. In the end, I hadn't done enough to keep him alive.

I walked the length of the street, passing no one on the way. Not only was I leaving this street forever, but soon enough nothing would remain of it. The fact literalized a feeling I sometimes had, that as I moved through the city, I was destroying what was behind me and inventing what was in front of me. I wandered out from the labyrinth of downtown streets and into the mathematical grid that made up the rest of the city. I passed the Baarle-Hertog building, and caught the sounds of a couple speaking German as they entered it. I thought I heard the word "Berlin," which reminded me of the newsreel I'd seen with Dora. That in turn made me think of other European cities, in particular London and Paris, both of which I'd visited in my youth. Various images jostled and overlapped in my mind. Ultimately, it occurred to me, cities were more alike than unlike—imperfect copies of each other. The real journeys were not between them but within them. Manhattan was an island so small that you could walk from east to west in forty minutes. On the other hand, it was infinite. Everyone thought they knew the midtown area, for example, with its plethora of famous landmarks. I'd even once lived in the neighborhood, and yet here I was on a street that was quite foreign to me.

I could feel myself drawn back into the world of Manne, as if to catch a last glimpse before it vanished for good. At a certain point, without my immediately realizing it, the cityscape

resolved itself into something recognizable. Here were stores
I'd once visited, restaurants I'd eaten at. The closer I got to
my old apartment block, the more I had the impression of
walking past dioramas of my former life, as if in a museum or
gallery. Even snatches of conversation from passersby started
to have a familiar ring to them. I was in a heightened state,
acutely aware of everything around me. Each bird in the sky,
each crack in the sidewalk rippled out into the world to make
it inevitable. And yet there remained an elusiveness. Gaps in
the purportedly seamless surfaces of reality.

There it was. Renovated, repainted, upgraded—itself but
not itself. As I gazed at the building, I felt flat and emotional
at the same time. I knew that if I waited long enough, Esterhazy would eventually appear. Somehow, he was still there,
despite everything that had happened, and all the changes to
the building. Perhaps he'd simply gravitated back to the place
where he'd first woken up into a new life. Perhaps the devel-
oper had searched him out, and had asked him if he'd wanted
his old apartment back, doubled in size now, having swallowed up its mirror image. Or perhaps there was yet another,
more sinister explanation.

I remembered being discharged from hospital, and finding
myself here, at this exact same spot, quite accidentally. I wondered now if at that moment, I'd simply walked back into my
apartment, I would have in fact walked back into Manne's life,
as if Esterhazy had never existed. Surely there was a world in
which events panned out exactly like that. Surely there were a
thousand such worlds, a thousand David Manneses. The one
who really had committed suicide in the subway, for instance.
Or the one who had never joined a college theater group, and
had therefore never met Abby. Each somehow contained and
implied all the others.

Esterhazy emerged into the lobby of my old apartment

block. He opened one of the mailboxes, quickly glanced through a letter, then put it back in its envelope and back in the mailbox. As he came out from the gates, I managed to get a good look at him. When he'd first reappeared outside my office, he'd seemed in a daze, not fully aware of the world around him. As if he'd just been fired from a job, or perhaps told that he had an incurable disease. Now he was different again. Tieless, his dark hair still damp and poorly combed, he looked haunted, harried, and yet determined at the same time.

The sun had climbed higher in the sky, its harsh light exposing the city with an implacable clarity. Despite the noise and movement of a city at work, the streets seemed strangely silent and static. I had the impression that the passing people might be actors, just as Esterhazy had once been an actor, and perhaps still was. He'd walked a few blocks in zigzag fashion, and was now disappearing down the subway steps at Lexington and Fifty-Ninth. He stopped for a second, and jerked his head around. His eyes scanned the crowd. Instinctively I pulled my hat over my eyes and made to hide behind the man in front of me. Had Esterhazy spotted me? There was little he could do about it, if he had. It was peak hour; the crowd was descending the stairs and surging through the tunnel onto the platform in a single stream. You couldn't swim against the current. Nonetheless, I thought I saw Esterhazy momentarily struggling to get back, before realizing that it was useless to try. But I could probably get to him, if I pushed my way ahead. Why would I want to do that? I felt the absolute necessity of speaking to Esterhazy, and at the same time the absolute impossibility of it.

We were on the downtown platform. That meant that Esterhazy wasn't going to Park Avenue. Maybe he was heading back to Penn Station. The train twisted its way along a curve, almost insect-like with its two beaming headlights. I was standing a row in from the edge. Esterhazy was there, just in front of me. We must have folded back onto each other, through some quirk of crowd dynamics. With the train only yards away, its lights dazzling me, I felt as if I were hurtling back to my own beginning. I raised my hands to Esterhazy's back. He twisted around in a sharp, single movement. I stared into him, for the first time. I could feel the warmth of his breath on my face. The slick film of Esterhazy's eyes seemed to project flickering scenes. Although I knew they were only reflections of the crowd behind me, they felt like images of a life, his or mine. Highly compressed, as in an intense and rapid dream.

Too late. If we'd spoken earlier, it might have been different. If I'd simply asked him for a light, then the manner of his reply might have revealed everything. We were the mysterious architects of each other's fate. Esterhazy let out a single cry, without echo or resonance, which died on his lips as he fell.

13

I looked up once again to the skyscrapers that dominated the mid-Manhattan skyline, awing the city's inhabitants into sub-mission. I was outside my office building again. Previously, there'd been an invisible barrier that had stopped me from going in, stranding me on the sidewalk bench opposite. Now this barrier was broken, smashed all to pieces. I made my way into the lobby. On the wall, opposite the front desk, were the brass plates—solid incarnations of tradition, respectability, dependability. In the past, whenever I'd entered the building, I'd glance over and see my name there, etched into one of them. It had never reassured me though; I'd always felt like an impostor. Reflexively I did the same thing now, looking over to the names, and seeing my own. DAVID F. MANNE, M.D. Yes, it was still there, recently polished even, gleaming. More real than it had ever been.

"Fourth floor, sir?"

"That's right."

The elevator operator looked up at me impassively,

registering no shock or surprise. Nothing at all. Just the old uncomfortable intimacy, as the elevator climbed through the floors, with its repertoire of mechanical clicks and whirls.

"Have a good day, sir."

"I will."

My office door again. The tiny brown scuff mark under the handle still visible, as it had been for years. And everything else resembling my memory of it. Once inside, I placed my hat and coat on the rack without even having to look, as I'd done so many hundreds of times before. My secretary glanced up from the letter she'd been typing. I could read a sort of horror on her face as I strode across the reception area and opened the door to my consulting room. There was my desk, with the typed pages neatly stacked to one side. I glanced at the title: "Notes on Untermeyer's conceptualizing of the transfer." I sat down, started looking through the pages, making the occasional correction. The phone came to life, its receiver shaking in the stand.

"David Manne?"

"Speaking."

"Jeff Speelman here. I guess . . ."

"It's about Abby, isn't it? I'm afraid I've already heard. Please accept my condolences."

I put the receiver back down. Outside the window on the ledge, a bird had built a nest, a swallow's nest, I thought. I could hear someone practicing the piano, a Beethoven sonata, on an upper floor. I gazed at the painting on the wall opposite my desk. It was of a female nude, voluptuous and most inappropriate. I'd go down to the Village and buy another canvas this very afternoon. It was a bright spring day after all, and I could feel a hint of warmth in the air, for the first time in many months.

ACKNOWLEDGMENTS

This novel owes a particular debt to John Franklin Bardin's *The Deadly Percheron* (Dodd, Mead, 1946). I have also adapted the occasional image or sentence from a number of other works, including *The Glamour* by Christopher Priest (Jonathan Cape, 1984), *Madness and Modernism: Insanity in the Light of Modern Art and Literature* by Louis Sass (Harvard Univeristy Press, 1994), *Autoportrait* and *Suicide* by Edouard Levé (P.O.L. 2005 and 2008) and the track *Clara* by Scott Walker (4AD, 2006).

Thanks to my family, in particular Patrick Wilcken for his critical reading of the text. Thanks also to Dennis Johnson, Taylor Sperry and Željka Marošević at Melville House.

And a very special thank you to Julie, for her all-round support and valuable editorial input.